SILVER

Over 100
Great Novels
of
Erotic Domination

If you like one you will probably like the rest

New Titles Every Month

All titles in print are now available from:

www.adultbookshops.com

If you want to be on our confidential mailing list for our Readers' Club Magazine (with extracts from past and forthcoming titles) write to:

SILVER MOON READER SERVICES

Shadowline Publishing Ltd
No 2 Granary House
Ropery Road
Gainsborough
DN21 2NS
United Kingdom

telephone: 01427 611697
Fax: 01427 611776

NEW AUTHORS WELCOME

Please send submissions to
Silver Moon Books
PO Box 5663
Nottingham
NG3 6PJ

Silver Moon is an imprint of Shadowline Publishing Ltd
First published 2008 Silver Moon Books
ISBN 1-904706-72-4
© 2008 Syra Bond

Fall from Grace

(True Confessions 2)

By

Syra Bond

Also by Syra Bond
True Confessions
Trojan Slaves
Trojan Whores

All characters in this book are fictitious, and any resemblance to real persons, living or dead, is purely coincidental.

This is fiction - In real life always practise safe sex!

1. Dawson's Rise
SERVITUDE OF A PENITENT

Father Dawson was a cruel confessor. If I was ever to be released it would be by his grace, and not until I had served my full penance, and I could not imagine when that time might come. Daily, I begged for mercy as he punished and tormented me. I crouched on my knees before him, my wrists bound, tears filling my eyes, pleading for forgiveness for crimes I did not even know I had committed. But he was slow to temper my misery and reluctant to offer his blessing. No, he made it clear with every blow — every smack, every cut of the whip or strap — that I must suffer at his hand until he decided I had endured enough. Until then, a shack alongside his little church — an oven of galvanised steel erected on a drift of sand in the Nevada desert — remained my prison.

Here, in this small metal shed — no more than a kennel, and built against the south facing back wall of his pathetic minster — I slept curled on the floor. Its low door was scorching hot and, when daily he took me out for punishment, I had to get down on my hands and knees and crawl through so that my shoulders and hips did not touch the frame. Its floor was a sheet of sand covered steel — I was never free of its grittiness against my sore skin. When I moved at night, unable to sleep because of the cold or the stinging pain left over from my daily chastisement, I felt its continual rasping abrasion. There was a narrow gap at the top of the door and this, for most of the time, was my only view of the world — a narrow slit of light and the parched scrubby desert beyond. Here, I crouched on my knees peering out, thinking only of freedom; freedom and its impossibility.

Weeks went by, the fearful monotony broken sometimes by a few circling vultures or the occasional squirming rattlesnake. The only people I saw were his few parishioners on a Sunday and, sometimes, on a weekday, the occasional supplicant who came for confession. These pathetic petitioners arrived at any time and, if my captor was not there, they waited, sitting in the heat of the sun, sometimes for hours until he returned. He did not attend to them quickly and often it was not until hours later, after he had eaten and fed me a bowl of grain, that he deigned to give his time to their case of repentance.

'Welcome to Dawson's Rise,' he would say wringing his hands together as finally he walked out to meet them. 'What sins do you have to declare, my children? Have I the power to forgive the terrible deeds which burden your souls? Or will your miserable transgressions, like those of my little captive, be beyond my ability?'

His black flowing robe twisted in slow circles around his sandaled feet and his starched white dog-collar flashed brightly in the unrelenting sun.

'Dawson's Rise' — I didn't know if it was named after my confessor, or he was named after it. All I knew was that it was a miserable cauldron of sizzling heat that burned from sunrise to sunset. For those long scorching hours — sweating, gasping for breath in my kennel — I felt it would never let up, then, almost immediately the sun went down, it became freezing cold.

Sometimes, perhaps feeling sorry for me, he left me a smelly grey blanket. I clutched it around my naked body, pushed it between my legs and pressed it against my face, as I curled up with my hands clasped around my knees in the hope of keeping some heat in my shivering body. In the depth of the night, watching through tear-stained eyes the stars twinkling beyond the gap above the kennel door, I listened to my teeth chattering. Most nights I cried. Sometimes I shouted to him for release. I screamed out that I could bear it no more — that my suffering was too much — but my pleading cries were always in vain, and the next morning it just began again.

When he let me out of my kennel — usually late on Sundays after his pathetic parishioners had finally left — he clipped a leash into a small padlock that hung from the leather collar he kept all the time around my neck. He kept the shining key to the padlock dangling from the black leather belt at his waist. Watching through the chink above the door, I used to see it flashing in the sunlight as he approached. I would imagine snatching it, releasing myself from his thrall and running free into the desert. Then I would think of the searing heat and being exposed in my nakedness to the burning sun, and in despair I would crouch again into the dark safety of the back of my kennel. No, I would never be free from this cruel captivity. I had lost all hope — I would never be free of my terrible enslavement to Father Dawson. My life would be forever spent suffering the humiliation of punishment, striving for my master's forgiveness, watching his penitents seeking his confessional.

Sometimes, I listened to him working on his shiny black Ford sedan. It had bright chrome wing mirrors and was kept in a dilapidated garage behind the church. He spent all his spare time in there. I heard him tinkering with spanners, revving the engine, sometimes I even imagined I could hear him stroking its shiny black surface as he walked around it admiringly. In service of this object, he demanded of his penitents — always keen to do his bidding — that they carry buckets of valuable water, filled from a leaky hose, to wash this prized possession and polish it with strongly scented wax. I saw them creeping past the door of my kennel, sweating, weighed down with water, unquestioningly doing as he ordered. I watched the plume of spray from the hose as it rose up in a fine hazy mist before quickly evaporating in the heat of the scalding sun. I could not believe how he wasted the precious liquid that for me only arrived every morning, strictly rationed to my barest needs, in a dirty cracked bowl. Another vehicle, an old Ford pick-up, received no attention and sat daily exposed to the sun rusty and covered in dust. I hated the sight of it — dark red with a wide toothy grill and a dirty white line down its side. It represented what I could not have — freedom.

'Where shall we walk today, my pet?' he would ask as if talking to a dog. 'Shall we take a stroll into the desert? Or perhaps you would prefer...' He would pause and rub his chin in mocking thought. '...yes, perhaps you would prefer the desert instead!'

His ridiculous joke amused him greatly, and he dribbled from his pale lips as he tugged on my lead and pulled me forward with a snatching yank. Sometimes I gulped and choked, sometimes I just winced in pain and denied him the pleasure of my suffering. But I could not resist that pleasure for myself. When he walked me, I dropped down against the collar and felt the tide of overwhelming humiliation that came with my posture. And my eyes rolled upwards as a shiver of joy went through me with the tightening of the collar. I always tried to suppress it at first, but I could not — every moment of shame and pain brought with it something delectable, something which filled me to overflowing with deep and uncontrollable joy. All the misery and disgrace to which I was subjected only fed my need for the pleasure it brought. I was caught in a trap — pain was my route to joy, and I craved joy more than anything in the world.

I crawled after him — afraid to do otherwise. If the lead fell slack he tightened it, if it tightened he judged me crawling too slowly and tugged it hard. Sometimes, when he did this, I was lifted up on the lead so that my arms dangled loosely from my shoulders. Sometimes, perhaps when the lead went suddenly tight around my neck, or the sting of his foot in my side took me by surprise, I cried out. If I did, he usually kicked me in the side again and then I knew to keep silent no matter how much pain I felt.

'Stop squeaking,' he would admonish. 'You sound like a pig. It will be the worse for you if you cannot discipline yourself against a trivial pain like that.'

Out in the open, the sun beat down on my bare back — he always kept me naked whether I was shut in the kennel or not— and the hot desert sand burnt the palms of my hands. I felt dizzy and exhausted. Sometimes I daydreamed, even hallucinated. I could not believe what had happened to bring me to such humiliating servitude — my involvement with Professor Harrington, his untimely death, my time with Dr Harris, and eventually, when I had thought there was no place to run, my escape and eventual imprisonment by the cruel torturer who now held me captive and claimed he would save my soul. What treachery he had dealt out to me. The indignity it might bring made me shiver with apprehension whenever I thought of it.

A trickle of spit oozed from the corner of my mouth. It ran down to the hot sand in a gluey strand. I dropped my head, licking at the spit, sucking it back up, feeling its frothy coolness against my lips. It broke free. My mouth felt dry. I closed my eyes in utter despair.

Again, he tugged the lead. I felt like holding back, resisting, just this once being defiant. My stomach filled with nerves as the thought raced through my mind — I could not stop myself. I dug my toes into the ground and felt the searing sand running between them. I dug them deeper. The burning sensation against my skin excited me. He yanked at the lead viciously. I gulped heavily and bit onto my lips. Another strand of spit spiralled down from my mouth. I kept my lips apart. Did I truly dare defy him?

'Can't keep up, eh?'

He yanked the lead again. I coughed and a spray of spit flew from between my open lips.

'We are not at the post yet. You are too quick to anticipate your pleasures, my little dog.'

I tried to stiffen my body. I tightened my shoulders and buttocks. He pulled again. I tightened more. I felt the excitement of my resistance. Another tug on the lead. A sharp pain in my neck. I tightened more. I felt the scorching heat of the sun on the taut skin of my buttocks. It was as though I had been lashed with a strap, as though my skin was reddened with the heat of a recent thrashing. A hot tingle of fresh delight ran through my body. I tightened my buttocks more and, this time, sensed the wetness that was beginning to run between the soft fleshy edges of my cunt. I tightened on it more. I felt the sides of my hot flesh squeezing together. Another shivering thrill passed through me. Again he yanked the lead — this time even harder. Again I choked, again I felt the pain, but now it was not in response to my torturer's hand — now, a new and delightful pleasure was now arising from deep within me. The pain he inflicted, the feeling of dread he passed to me through the yanking lead, they were not what made me follow him in obedience. No, it was not the threat of pain and punishment, it was the delight within me that the pain set off, the excitement aroused by the thought of what he would inflict which made me tense myself for more.

'Ah, look, my little Syra. There is the post. Crawl to it. Go on. Crawl to it, my little malefactor. You know it is the place where your sins are surrendered. You know it is where you want to be.'

I saw the post against the blinding sun — a thick four by four stump about waist high driven deep into the blistering sand. A heavy leather leash hung from a large iron link screwed into its top.

I pulled forward. He was not dragging me now — I was not hanging back as he yanked at the lead to draw me on. The sight of the post, its solid unforgivingness, the shiny leather surface of the dangling leash flashing in the bright sunlight, the heavy buckle at its end — these were all I saw. And the sight of them made me pull with an eagerness released by my anticipation of the promise they held.

'Back, my eager pet! Back!'

I felt like a dog, pulling against the restraining hand of its master — single minded, eager, and undaunted by admonishment.

'Back! Back!'

He yanked the lead and smacked its edge against my naked back.

'Back!'

He pulled me so hard I twisted in the air and fell back, panting and confused.

Foaming spit ran from my mouth. It dribbled down my chin and I felt its bubbling heat as it dried in the baking sun. But I could not hold myself back. I strained forward impatiently and, this time, but on a tight lead, he let me approach the post.

I dug my fingers and toes into the sand as I pulled forward. My nostrils flared.

'You are so eager today, my little penitent. Perhaps during the night you have realised more of the sins that still hide within you. It is so rewarding to me to help you seek forgiveness for them.'

He bent down and stroked his hand across my upturned buttocks. He let his fingers slip between them. He probed their tips against the swollen wet flesh of my cunt. I pressed back against them, and felt them slipping in on the moisture that glistened on the surface of my hot crack.

He pulled them out and smacked my buttocks with his hand. I lurched forward.

I waited by the post and laid my cheek against its hard surface. I looked up at him. I needed his permission, I had learned that much.

'May I, father?' I asked, beseeching him with my tear-filled eyes.

He paused, slackened the lead slightly and smiled.

'Oh, my child, my dearest Syra, you have so much sin. It is such a long road ahead for you. There is so much to forgive.'

I did not listen, I had only one thing on my mind — the post and what delights it would bring.

'Father, have I your permission? Must I pray first? I am already on my knees. See how I beg for your permission. Yes, must I pray? Tell me my prayer, father, tell me my prayer.'

'If it was only so easy, my child. If only a simple prayer could bring about your salvation. But yes, let us pray, though a single prayer is a drop in the ocean of your sins. Yes, let us pray.'

I sat upright on my knees, brought my hands together and dropped my head. I felt the sudden heat of the sun against the back of my bare neck.

Father Dawson lifted the hem of his robe slightly and knelt beside me. He put his hands together, looked up into the cloudless sky and spoke in a clear distinct voice.

'I bring this penitent again, oh Lord. There is no end to her sins, and so no end to her punishment. Her life is a devotion to forgiveness, but I fear she will never find it. I can only hope your patience is not overly tried.'

He sighed heavily.

'Now, say these words after me, my child.'

I licked my lips.

'Lord, I have sinned greatly,' he said.

'Lord, I have sinned greatly,' I responded.

Just speaking the words sent a shiver of joy through my body. I pulled myself as upright as possible. The tension in my buttocks tightened against the soft flesh of my cunt. Immediately, I felt its silky wetness and tightened more.

'I am still a poor sinner.'

'I am still a poor sinner.'

I felt the aching tightness in my nipples as they hardened and extended at the sound of the words.

'I must suffer more every day to even hope that I can be saved.'

'I must suffer more everyday to even hope that I can be saved.'

I felt my dry lips moistened by the soft wetness of spit

as it bubbled between them. I licked it back into my mouth and swallowed it. I pressed my hands together as tightly as I could. I licked my tongue out again, this time letting the flat of its pink surface first touch then lick against the timber post.

Father Dawson watched me. I flushed with embarrassment. I felt as though I had been caught out, but I could not stop.

'Even as I beg your forgiveness, Lord, I commit more sins.'

'Even as I beg your forgiveness, Lord, I commit more sins.'

I kept licking.

'Lord, see how your evil sinner falls victim to her carnal needs.'

'Lord, see how your evil sinner falls victim to her carnal needs.'

I pressed my tongue against the hard wooden edge of the post.

'Place me into the hands of your servant, oh Lord.'

'Place me into the hands of your servant, oh Lord.'

'Let him do with me as he sees fit.'

'Let him do with me as he sees fit.'

I sniffed at the spit as it spread from my tongue onto the timber of the post.

'Let him bring me to the point where I can suffer no more — the point of exquisite delight where pain and ecstasy unite.'

'Let him bring me to the point where I can suffer no more — the point of exquisite delight where pain and ecstasy unite.'

I licked feverishly.

'Let him plan out my ascent of this summit, oh Lord,

and lead me over all the obstacles that presently stand in the way of my ultimate grace.'

'Let him plan out my ascent of this summit, oh Lord, and lead me over all the obstacles that presently stand in the way of my ultimate grace.'

I was drooling uncontrollably. Spit was running down my chin and dripping onto my hard, aching nipples. I pressed them against the post, against its sharp edge. My knees felt weak. I dropped my hands to my sides. I wanted to delve my fingers between my legs, to draw them along my crack, to release all its gleaming wetness, to feel its flesh swelling, throbbing, expecting. But I did not. I waited. It was time for my punishment and, although I could barely wait for it to begin, the tension of waiting and the knowledge of what was to follow, controlled my desires to do otherwise.

I trembled in anticipation. I stared down at my aching nipples — they throbbed, hard and prominent. I wanted them sucked. I wanted to see spit dripping from their straining ends. Then I wanted them pinched — so hard, so fiercely, so cruelly that tears streamed down my face. And I wanted them thrashed, with a strap or a belt — something with a hard cutting edge, something that would bring the highest levels of pain, and something that would release my uncontrolled screams. I wanted to feel the tension in them straining against the smacking sting of a viciously wielded strap. I wanted to feel them on fire. I wanted them bitten. I wanted to feel the cutting edges of sharp teeth eating into their throbbing flesh. And I wanted to beg for it all to stop, knowing that it would not and knowing that, in truth, I wanted it to continue.

Father Dawson stood up. I did not look at his face. He did not allow it at this time. This was the time of complete obedience — the moment that tested my commitment to his will. No, I did not dare look at his face.

I did not move as he unclipped the leash from my collar — something else I had learnt at his hand. This was a moment of freedom, and I had to show him that, even when I was not secured, I was still under his control.

He took hold of the shiny leather strap that was fixed to the post and clipped it into the large iron link at its top. I breathed quickly and licked back the spit from my chin. What else could I do? It was impossible to hide the thrill of anticipation that was coursing through my veins. I wanted to urge him to wind the strap more quickly into the collar at my neck. I wanted to plead with him to draw my neck up against the hard edge of the post tighter than ever before. I wanted him to make me more secure than I had ever felt. I wanted to hang against the unforgiving post, limp yet constrained, captive and hopeless. I just wanted…

'Onto all fours,' he ordered curtly.

Sometimes he let me get onto my hands and knees without this order, just sometimes, but not this time. I could sense the urgency in his voice. This time he was not prepared to wait. This time he only wanted to see me punished, he did not want to engage in the moments that might precede it — the waiting, the pent-up excitement, the wondering, the expectation.

'On all fours!' he shouted again. I had made him wait, and he was angry, and that meant he would be even more severe with me than usual.

I did as he ordered. I dipped my back, allowing it to curve downwards from my shoulders and rise up again to my taut exposed buttocks. I felt the searing heat of sun on my skin. I forced my buttocks higher; they opened enough to expose the soft oval of flesh that was my cunt. The heat of the blazing sun was intense — it burned like a branding iron against the swelling delicate flesh. I felt moisture running in the crack. I widened my buttocks more — the edges of my flesh pulled against the tension. I dropped my head forward and swallowed heavily in a massive gulp.

'Yet more sins,' he sighed. 'Always more. The unending flow of your sinfulness is sometimes too much to witness. Yes, even for a minister of the Lord. Even with God's support, my dearest Syra, sometimes your evil is too much to bear.'

I wanted to tell him how sorry I was. I wanted to plead with him to help me, to save me, to release my sinfulness, but I knew that although there might be a right time, this was not it. In the night, when I was alone and curled up in my kennel — when I had no greater pleasure to distract me — then there was nothing else in my life except the desire for forgiveness. At these times, that was all that mattered. But now, at this moment, my desire to beg and my being able to do nothing else except beg were brought together by my single-minded anticipation of the pain to come.

The thought of it made me gasp. I opened my mouth wide. Spit ran down between my legs. I watched it dribbling towards the sand. My eyes followed its bubbly strand. I wondered if it would reach the sand before my punishment started. I had no time to think before the answer was given — 'No'.

2. DAWSON'S RISE
MY SUFFERING AT THE POST

Father Dawson yanked me up tightly to the post. My head banged against its hard edge. I felt dizzy. I looked towards my kennel — as if its rickety frame might offer some sense of safety. The leaking hose they used for cleaning the black Ford sedan lay in a tangle on the sand. Water sprayed in a fine multicoloured mist from its heavy brass end. I licked my lips at the thought of its cooling sanctity, and imagined myself lying beneath its soft mist, naked, my legs wide, saturated by its soothing rain.

Two of Father Dawson's shabby penitents had arrived for his absolution. They sat together on the rusty front bumper of the old Ford pickup. They were young but troubled. I could see they had done something, committed some wrongdoing, and were here in the hope that my cruel master would somehow wash it away. I could see in their eyes the hope that, with the power invested by God in his hands, he would grant them forgiveness for something for which they should more rightly be punished with a cruelty beyond even Father Dawson's means. They both wore blue dungarees, had been talking quietly and picking up and throwing pebbles to amuse themselves. Now they could not keep from staring at me — captive, naked, lashed to the post and awaiting a punishment for something they could not understand.

Behind them, stood an old woman, her craggy face worn by years exposed in the desert sun. Her tangled black hair hung in greasy strands on her naked shoulders. Her breasts were exposed and the light shift that draped from her bony hips barely covered the dark triangular shape of her pubic hair. She squeezed up her eyelids tightly, lifted her hands and beckoned me — it was a cruel gesture. I pulled against the collar at my neck. I wanted to spit at her for her spitefulness. I thought I saw her smile, but I could not distinguish it from a sneer.

I hung on the leash that connected the collar at my neck to the top of the thick post. I knew he was going to beat me — a thrashing of some sort, a whipping perhaps, or maybe a caning. I never knew exactly what it would be, but I knew it would be painful, and I knew that, even before it finished, I would have confessed all I knew. But it never stopped there — simple confession was never enough to halt the pain at his hands. He would continue long after I had stopped begging for mercy. He was never content until he saw me lift up my buttocks against the pain — not in spite of it, but lift myself to meet it, to welcome it. He was never satisfied until I begged further, until my salivating lips and drooling tongue cried out for more — more pain, more savagery, more humiliation. And even then, he would not release me, even when I opened my legs wide, even when I lifted my cunt to the whip or the cane, even when I screamed uncontrollably as he lashed my tender exposed flesh unendingly, even when I shuddered with ecstasy, when I licked at the parched sand, when I crawled and licked his shoes, when I clung onto his legs and entreated him to lash me even harder, even then, when I did all these things, still he did not stop. And it never seemed to end. He thrashed me into oblivion. The lashing strap, or cutting cane, would still be lacing my buttocks well after I had slumped before him, overcome with the pain he had inflicted so cruelly, barely able to keep myself conscious enough to know that there was still more to come.

Yes, he was the cruellest master — the most unforgiving

torturer. He drove me to the pinnacle of pain as, at the same time, he raised me to the heights of pleasure. The two came together — I was both a victim to his cruelty and to my own primitive need for the pleasure it brought. As I was racked with anguish and suffering so I was seized with the shivering ecstasy of the deepest joy. As I begged to be saved from the humiliation he bestowed on me, so I shivered with pleasure at the delight it transmitted to every part of my trembling body. But all the suffering, all the joy, had exhausted me, drained me, left me now unable to cope. I did not think I could stand any more. Even the delectability of the highest joys was no longer enough for me to tolerate the pain and disgrace that was the route to it. His devious and savage cruelty had overcome me. The pleasures I had experienced had given over to abject suffering — now I could only think of freedom.

I looked up into the relentless sun — a flaming fire in the cloudless sky. Its heat burned my forehead and cheeks and, when I closed my eyes, its brightness and radiance lit up my eyelids so that all I saw was dazzling spots of intense yellow light.

The two ragged penitents came up and stood one on each side of me. For a moment I felt the relief of being in their shade.

'Something different for you today, my little pet,' said Father Dawson, as he stalked around me holding his forefinger against his nose. 'Something to help shake out your sins and allow you a complete confession. Oh, how relieved you will be if you are emptied of them. And I will be overjoyed with your salvation.'

His sneering tone made me shiver — his words were more ominous than usual. A wave of fear ran through me. I bit hard onto my lips — an introduction to the pain to come.

'Untie her!' he ordered.

I slumped to the ground as the leash was released. I was no longer secured, and there was a sense of relief, but I knew it was not freedom. I tried to crawl back to the post — there was safety in its harsh unforgiving strength, and I was too exposed away from it. I stretched my hands out to it. Father Dawson's foot stepped across by clawing hands and pressed them down into the soft hot sand.

I looked up. The sun was behind his head. A halo of blazing gold shone around him. I fell back terrified. He was like an apparition.

'Please,' I begged. 'I can stand no more.'

He laughed cruelly.

'But you must, my little pet. There is so much more to come. How can you deny yourself pleasures that you have not yet experienced?'

He nodded to his assistants.

Each penitent put a hand beneath each of my armpits and lifted me upwards. It was a relief to feel their strength holding me up — there was something strangely comforting about it.

One of them sniggered. I looked up at him — he was unshaved, scraggy and wide eyed. He laughed as he caught my gaze and squeezed my upper arm painfully in his tightening grip. I felt his cruelty. A gold tooth shone behind his half open lips. It glistened with spit from his hot squirming tongue, as it caught the light from the ever present, searing sun.

I did not know whether to cry out or not. I wanted to, I needed to, but I knew there was more suffering to come and that saving my cries for mercy until later would help calm the flames of pain that would then be burning in my body. Yes, I knew that what was ahead would have a more rightful claim to my screams. I bit harder onto my lips and fought the reflex need to shout out. Yes, I would save my cries.

The one with the gold tooth let go of my arm and spun around. He stood before me looking down as the other held me on my knees before him.

I looked up into his face. I realised how pitiful I was — my eyes wide and appealing, my mouth slightly open, my lips trembling with confusion and expectation of what was to come. I inclined my head slightly to the side, asking him to forgive me for something I had not even done. I felt a wave of shame.

He grinned and his gold tooth flashed. I winced and pulled back. I felt a sharp pain under my arms as the other gripped me tightly and pushed me back into place. Yes, I was in place, in the place they wanted me, under their control, and these disciples were in turn under the control of Father Dawson. I felt his dominating hand even as I knelt before his grinning acolyte.

I thought again of reaching for the post. I felt my body tensing as it prepared itself. I imagined grabbing the post's hard edges and offering myself to its strength. I thought of them clipping my collar to it, holding me against it, pinioning me tightly to it. And I imagined myself cowering at it, crying out in agony as the lash came down time after time on my upturned naked buttocks and back. I saw myself writhing beneath the thrashing leather, twisting and turning helplessly as my skin was reddened and striped by its unforgiving ferocity. I felt the overpowering call of the sanctity of pain that it promised — a pain I knew, a humiliation that would satisfy me with its painful disgrace. But I knew I could not move — it was a ridiculous fantasy. I had no choice — I must await whatever he had planned for me.

I was held fast on my knees. The penitent who stood before me grinned again. He opened the front of his trousers, pushed his hand inside them and drew out his cock. It was thick and engorged. Its end throbbed and, as he pushed it towards my face, I felt its heat.

He pressed the hot glans against my lips. I looked up at him.

He nodded.

'Between your lips first,' he drawled. 'Make it wet and let me feel your tongue around it. Draw your lips tight and run them along its shaft. When you have done this to my satisfaction, I will tell you what I want next.'

I looked quickly to the side. I did not know if I should take instructions from him. I felt I must have Father Dawson's approval before I did anything.

I was snatched back to face the penitent.

'I have given you your orders! Do as I have said!'

I sensed his anger. I looked again — still I felt afraid of acting without my master's approval. This time I was snatched back more viciously. The one behind me clasped his hands against my cheeks and squeezed them tightly, forcing my pursed lips towards the others waiting cock.

'Do what I have said! Your master has given you to us. He has no more need of you. He says you are beyond his help. Do as I say!'

I felt a great tide of fear rise within me. I could not believe I had been abandoned. I leant forward until the hot glans touched my lips. I opened my lips and let them enfold it. It tasted sweet, and it was hot and hard. I licked it, taking saliva from beneath my tongue and using its tip to spread my spit across the throbbing end. I sucked at the hot glans, drawing it in, and, as it entered, I felt the ribs of the venous shaft against the insides of my cheeks.

I looked up at the penitent. He stared down at me, his eyes commanding me, regulating my movements, forcing me to follow his instructions.

'Now, take it down!'

I felt his cock's heavy end against the back of my throat. As it touched I felt myself gag. My throat closed and I felt an irresistible nauseous heave. I relaxed, my throat opened and the heaving sensation passed. I drew it further. I welcomed it into my throat and, as saliva flooded around it, I swallowed on it, pulling it in as much as it would go until his heavy testicles were splayed and pressed against my spit-smeared chin.

I felt the gagging sensation again. I could not stop my throat tightening on the pulsating shaft. My babbling breath gurgled past the ribs of his hard cock. Bubbling spit squeezed up along it and frothed out in a foamy, gluey mass around my lips and down my chin. I sucked in and again my throat tightened, this time more, and I felt his heavy cock expanding as his semen ran up the throbbing shaft.

It splashed into my throat and I choked. Gulping and gasping, I kept it in, tasting the hot semen, swallowing it, sucking it down. He pulled back and his still flowing semen filled my mouth, covering my tongue, and sticking to my teeth before flooding out over my bottom lip and down my chin.

A hand behind me forced me forward. I dropped onto all fours. The cock above me still flowed with semen, splashing more of it onto the back of my head and around one of my ears. It trickled down the side of my face and over my cheek.

A sudden smack on my buttocks made me twist sidewards. I looked around but another vicious smack told me to turn back. Another sharp smack and I realised that the penitent behind me was driving me forward with the open palm of his hand. Another smack told me to continue, another told me to move more quickly.

Semen ran from my mouth as I crawled forward across the searing sand. I stared ahead. A rainbow of light dazzled me. Smack after smack drove me on. I swallowed and felt more of the sticky semen running down my throat. Another smack and I turned my buttocks up to meet it — the sharp sudden hit, the penetrating sting, the sound, the feeling of obedience all came together and made me want it more. I dropped my shoulders lower so that the small of my back dipped down and accentuated the rising mounds of my reddened buttocks. Another smack, another sharp sting, another instruction and a wave of painful, humiliating pleasure flooded through me.

I crawled towards the rainbow. It was formed in the mist of water spraying from the brass end of the leaky hose. I pulled myself into it. Another smack slapped wetly as my buttocks were drenched by the cloud of misty spray.

There were no more smacks. I stopped — a moment of relief was my order to wait. I stayed there, on my hands and knees in the middle of the mist of spray that rose in a circling plume from the hose. It cooled my skin. I bathed in it. It was luxurious. I swallowed heavily on the semen in my mouth — it was delectable. I lifted my buttocks and let the water droplets collect and run down their crack. Their cool moisture ran around my anus. It dilated with the contact and a deep tingling sensation flowed up into my bowels. It flowed down against the soft flesh of my cunt and its pliable tissue swelled in response to its soft caress.

I raised my face into the gentle storm of water from the hose. The spray ran into my wide open eyes, down my cheeks and into my gaping mouth. It mixed with the semen which still clung to my lips and it ran inside and mixed with the semen that still stuck to my tongue and lips. The misty water brought a new freshness to my mouth and I tasted the semen anew — more aromatic, more salty, more delectable than even before. I felt the heat in my cunt and I lifted my buttocks as high as I could, exposing my crack to the cloud of coolness and the soft touch of its delicate rain.

Suddenly, my hands were grabbed. My face fell against the wet sand. It stuck to my lips and I tasted its gritty bitterness on my tongue. They dragged me up and bound my hands together with a spare piece of hose. I was confused and could not make out what was happening to me. They lashed the old piece of hose that held my hands together around the rusty front bumper of the old pick-up. They pulled my feet off the ground and stretched me across the long sharp front wing. They held my legs apart. I saw myself in the wing mirror that was immediately in front of my face. I shrunk back from what I saw — tear-filled eyes, sand mixed with the semen stuck to my cheeks and nose, water dripping down from my spit smeared lips.

Suddenly, I screamed in pain. A lashing cut across my buttocks made my body go rigid as a spare piece of rubber hose was brought down stingingly across them. It came down again. I reared back against the bonds that held my wrists and cried out in agony. Spit and semen exploded from my mouth and sprayed up into the multicoloured rain of mist from the hose that enshrouded me.

Another lashing blow from the hose came down

viciously against my taut skin. Again I reared back, again I screeched out, but before I could recover, I felt another cutting blow, and I cried out with another bubbling scream. And it did not stop as the flexing rubber pipe struck the swollen edges of my cunt. The pain pierced my convulsing body. I felt burned from the inside. It was agony. I shrieked.

Then suddenly, as quickly as the thrashing had started, it stopped. The mist of spray around me subsided, the rainbow cleared, the heat of the sun again burst through.

Gasping for breath, I looked at myself in the mirror. My hair was wet and tangled, my face was dripping, my mouth was open, and my lips were trembling. As I watched myself, I saw my face relax; recovering from the beating with the hose, hoping it was all over. Then it all changed. In the mirror I saw my mouth gape stiffly; my eyes open wide, and my whole face tense as a fresh and terrifying scream issued from deep within me.

I tightened my buttocks as I felt a bursting spray of water between them. It stung my skin sharply as its pressured jet forced the spraying water against it. Then it was placed against my anus — open and exposed. I wriggled to try and get away but it was impossible, my legs were held tightly, my hands bound, my body stretched prone across the metal wing of the pick-up.

I could not resist it. The brass nozzle of the hose went inside. I felt a bubbling fullness as its spray shot into my rectum. I dropped my jaw and watched my face as the water filled me — cold, penetrating, surging. My watching eyes followed all the movements on my face in the mirror as slowly I was filled to overflowing. When my rectum could take no more, I felt the water bursting out between my anal ring and the tightly crammed brass fitting. I licked my tongue out. I could not stop it. I let go of everything I was. My cunt was seized with heat. A massive wave of joy came over me — it filled me, terrified me and was released in me at the same time. My body went rigid. My face in the mirror horrified me — my staring eyes and wide mouth testifying to the mixture of fear, terror and pleasure that came together in a seizing ecstasy that burst inside me in a massive overwhelming explosion.

I listened to the bubbling sounds as the brass nozzle was taken away. A fresh mist burst around me and, as it picked up the multicoloured threads of the rainbow, another surging tide of ecstasy ran through my trembling body. Uncontrollably, I shook all over.

I stared into the spray. I saw the old woman on the other side. She held something bright in one hand and beckoned me with the other.

The tension at my wrists was released and I felt the grip on my ankles removed. I slid off the bonnet of the pickup and fell to the ground in a shivering heap. I could hardly get my breath. Semen still dripped from my mouth, water from the hose ran down the insides of my thighs.

I saw something glittering. I squinted my tear-filled eyes. It was a key! It must have been dropped on the ground by one of my tormentors. I slid further down and covered it with my hand. My mind was suddenly filled. Could I take it? Did I dare? Could I run? Yes! Yes, I could!

The next thing I knew, I dropped, gasping for breath, onto the hot red and cream coloured plastic seat of the pick-up. Suddenly I saw the old woman at the open passenger window. Spit dribbled from her cracked lips. I fumbled trying to get the key into the ignition.

She reached her bony hand in through the window and dropped open the glove box. It was full of dollar bills.

'Seek the young girl,' she hissed. 'She will lead you into the mist. Go with her and your sins will be washed away.'

I stared at her. I could not move. I was frozen with fear.

'Go! Go, my child!' she screeched. 'Your spirit is waiting to be set free. Go!'

My hands shook as I struggled to twist the key in the ignition. Then I heard the noisy V8 growl. I rammed the shift into 'drive', grabbed the huge, dished, plastic steering wheel and the old Ford lurched forward. I held my breath, leant forward and stabbed my foot into the accelerator. The old pick-up tore off in a billowing cloud of dust down the god-forsaken dirt road that seemed to lead to nowhere. I was in a blind panic. I did not even notice I was naked.

I glanced only once in the rear view mirror. The old woman stood crouched where I had left her. I saw a figure approach her and press something into her hand. The figure was swathed in a long black robe and the white collar at his neck flashed in the bright light of the glaring desert sun. It was Father Dawson. I did not care. I knew in my heart that I should, but I did not care. I was free!

3. HALL OF MIRRORS, NEW MEXICO
THE OLD INDIANS STORY

I just stared through the windscreen and drove as fast as I could. I felt in a dream for hours. Finally, when I looked away from the road ahead, I saw the twinkling key from Father Dawson's belt lying on the passenger seat. The old woman had left it for me!

I took the collar from my neck and threw it from the window. Later that night, when I stopped to sleep, I pulled an old blanket over me. I found a pair of jeans and a T shirt beneath it. I couldn't believe my luck — it was as though everything had been arranged!

The next day, I crossed the old Butterfield Coach line from Arizona into New Mexico. I began to relax. Yes, it was true! I had escaped the clutches of Father Dawson!

I drove on into the desert. Huge hoardings advertised any novelty an isolated township held in esteem and thought would cause a passer-by to stop — the amazing 'ant-baby', a collection of letters from aliens, the skeleton of a giant mouse. Looking to buy a bottle of water, I called in at the museum in Whites City and went to see the 'mummified cliff-dwelling baby'. I thought it macabre, placed as it was in its primitive wrapping next to the 'Win-o-lot' fruit machine. It sounded exceptional on the notice outside, but it was the same as everything so eagerly vaunted on the road by gaudy signs — not as spectacular as announced. The other exhibits — the world's only albino rattlesnake, a giant saucepan, a huge ball of string, the remains of a wolf-child — all turned out to be something smaller, simpler or less vicious.

The bottle of water I bought was caked with dust and the top was loose. When I swigged it, it tasted of sand.

Desert was followed by more desert, emptiness by increasing isolation. The remoteness made everything stand out as extraordinary — a Honda Gold Wing, an exceptionally tall yucca, a gigantic organ pipe cactus, a crazed road runner — and everything, simple or exceptional, sizzled beneath the relentless sun. In a roadside shack with a torn film of perforated zinc for a door, I bought a pair of white panties incongruously displayed on a dusty counter top with tins of baked beans and dinosaur bones.

I ate outside a wooden shack with a glowing neon 'open' sign above the door. Beside it, an incongruously gaudy car wash flashed its pink and purple message into the searing heat — 'Big Dog's 24 Hour Cactus Car Wash'.

I had hot tea with sour milk which, in the end, I had to make myself at a dirty sink inside the stuffy shack. An Indian headdress and brightly coloured beads hung from the old bent roof trusses. The walls were decked with artefacts for sale — feathers, moccasins, a carved peace pipe, rugs and blankets with brash diagonal designs, bracelets and necklaces, decorated leather belts with silver and turquoise buckles.

The old Indian who ran the café erected a make-do sun shelter out of string and a blanket above my table — the only one and barely able to support itself on its rickety legs. He pushed his leg against my thighs as he worked and once his arm glanced against my breasts when he dropped the grey tangle of knotted string on the ground. In the end, he pulled the contraption up tight. I welcomed its shade and sat back on the wobbly chair.

Straight away, he drew up a stool and sat forward with his hands clasped between his bony knees.

'You've never been here before. I can tell,' he said.

'You look pale. Here, drink your tea.' He motioned towards my cup. 'Drink it all. It will revitalise you. Help you to see things right. The desert is a mysterious place. It contains strange things. Here, drink your tea.'

I sipped my tea. It tasted odd — musty and stale — but I was thirsty and needed it.

The old Indian brought his face close to mine. I imagined I saw figures in his blood shot eyes. I smiled at my silly imagination and immediately realised my lips were numb. I rubbed them with my hand and could not feel them! I could not feel my hand either!

'I'll tell you about some of the mystifying things that happen here, in the desert,' he said, now touching my knees with his hands.

I started to feel dizzy, dreamy — nothing looked right. Everything was confused — the wrong colour, jagged at the edges, fragmented. I thought I reached out my hand, but saw that it did not move. I spoke, but there was no sound. I knew I was hot, but I could not feel the heat. I felt detached and fearful. Everything around me looked misshapen and deformed. My stomach filled with nerves.

In a low, hypnotic voice, the old Indian began to tell me a story. Hoping the sensations I was experiencing would pass off, I listened as well as I could.

'The Navajo used to live in these parts, bordered to the north by the Ute and to the south by the Apache. They were famous as blanket weavers and feared as fierce warriors. Their men were reputed as the bravest of all native Indians in battle. Although they had one leader, there were many small groups, often renegades bent on robbery and killing, and each of these small bands had its own chief. The most famous around here was Aquila — the Great Eagle. His ferocity knew no bounds — he was cruel, vengeful and fearless. They say his cry could be heard for miles. His teeth were capped with gold found in the hills north of Carlsbad, and he had a huge eagle tattooed on his chest which was so complex and exact that, it is said, at night the eagle flew free of its master's body. Sometimes, they say, the magnificent bird could be seen perched at the top of a great waterfall calling out to the spirits of the mist, asking them to give up the souls of those who had been lost in the waters of the river.'

I wanted to reach out to touch him. To tell him I felt frightened. I imagined my hand stretching out to him, but it disappeared as I watched it.

He pushed his hands between my legs, probing forward until his fingers touched the bottom of the zip of my creased up jeans. I thought of myself squirming away from his groping hands but, when I tried, nothing happened — I was helpless.

'Aquila suffered a terrible fate. The gods banished him to wander the earth forever until he put right the wrong that he had done them — until he found a replacement for the woman he had stolen from them. She was a Choktaw named Telulah, which means 'leaping water'. She was brought from Louisiana by French traders and stolen as booty by Aquila in a raid on the trader's encampment. The beautiful Telulah was washed from her canoe above the great waterfall. She clung to a branch at its top crying out for help. Aquila took pity on her and, risking his own life, rescued her from the thundering waters. But the gods had already claimed her and were angry that their prize had been stolen from them.'

'A few days later, a raiding party stole Telulah and she spent the rest of her days as a captive — punished and tortured by cruel young braves who kept her continually bound, on her knees and secured with a collar and lead. She was beaten daily, whipped and thrashed with canes, burned with brands and used for every sexual pleasure they could think of. They say she took the cocks of all the braves in her cunt, her anus and her mouth every day and sometimes, for many days at a time, she fed only on their semen. Once they dangled her over a waterfall on a rope and, for bets, themselves fought amongst the wild waters to penetrate her. It is told that several of them hung onto her at one time as the waters threatened to drown them all. But, throughout her suffering, so it is said, she thought only of Aquila and, because of her faithful devotion to him, she never experienced a moment of pleasure. No matter what delights she was offered, she never again felt her own joy for the rest of her life. The gods came to Aquila and, as a punishment for their loss, they demanded he walk the earth forever until he found them a replacement for the beautiful Telulah — someone who they could punish and who, like Telulah, would never find pleasure in any of the punishments they used on her. Since this time, he has found many and tested them all but, unlike Telulah, they have never resisted the call of pleasure and so Aquila's wanderings continue.'

I felt a shiver run through me but I could tell that now there was no reaction in my body at all.

I saw the old Indian's hand working its way along the zip of my jeans, feeling all the links — picking at them with his nails one by one. Then he moved his clawing fingers up across my stomach to my breasts. He cupped each of them in his hands before slowly inscribing circles around them with his fingertips. He pinched my nipples, slowly, one by one — I felt the pain but could not pull back. He reached up to my face. I could not turn away.

He stroked my cheeks, cocked his head and looked deeply into my unblinking eyes. He grinned knowingly.

Suddenly, from nowhere, I sensed figures around me — somehow I could feel the heat of their bodies. I smelled their odour — I could tell they were men. I felt myself lifted up. Yes, I was being lifted up — borne on their shoulders. My head dropped to the side. I realised it was night. I saw flares and burning torches. I tried desperately but still I could not move. I felt as if I might fall at any moment. I imagined putting my hands out to save myself but nothing happened. Then, as quickly as I had been picked up, I was lowered down. They laid me on a cold stone platform. It was an altar! I saw them stand back. I stared up at the stars — I could do nothing else.

Then I sensed hands around my waist, undoing the zip of my jeans. Then I felt the tugging pressure against my hips as they were pulled down. My body arched upwards as they lifted my buttocks off the altar to free my jeans. My thin white panties came down with them, twisting to start with into the crack of my cunt before they were yanked free. I imagined myself crying out as my flesh was pulled roughly by the wound-up material, but I could not open my mouth nor make any sound. I could only imagine my nakedness and humiliating exposure as, finally, my panties were pulled off over my feet. They wrenched my T shirt over my head, lifting it roughly then dropping it down with a bang against the hard surface of the altar top. My eyes went misty for a moment. I thought of myself holding the back of my head in my hands and shouting out in pain and shock, but again nothing happened — my body was limp, I was completely unable to move or make any sound.

A man in a multi-coloured mask and a feathered

headdress leant forward and stared down at me. He probed my mouth with his fingers and pulled the tip of my tongue forward with his thumb and forefinger. I felt the need to choke, to vomit, but I just looked up weakly into his peering eyes as he pulled and pinched my tongue harder.

He stood back and yelled something — a whooping cry. I could not understand what it might mean, but it was ominous and its shrill sound filled me with terror.

I sensed movement behind him — something flashing, something bright.

I lay on my back on the stone altar, naked, unable to move, unable to cry out, unable to react to anything — I was terrified, filled with an uncontrollable but inexpressible anxiety.

The brightness appeared again. A sudden flash of light engulfed me. I stared helplessly into its glare. Then I saw myself! My body ran with a tide of fear. I saw myself lying on the altar! I felt dizzy with confusion. I couldn't understand what was happening. I thought I'd lost my mind.

I saw myself getting closer — tilting, tipping, all the time flashing brightly. The image twisted and gyrated then, as it came to a halt, I saw what it was. It was a huge polished mirror, a massive shield of some kind. It was being held above me, showing me an image of my helpless, exposed body. Another wave of fear came over me. Seeing myself like this made me realise afresh the awful situation I had found myself in.

Hands behind my shoulders made me sit up. I stared down between my legs which had been forced open and drawn up. My knees were splayed wide, and my naked crack was exposed to the reflective mirror, its pink slit glistening wet and slightly parted. The base of the slit ran into the darker centre of my anus. I saw my face staring back — drawn and pale. And I saw my tongue, lying loosely over my bottom lip — limp and lifeless, pink and exposed. My eyes were black — my pupils dilated across their whole width. My hair was wet and straggly and beads of sweat ran down my cheeks and across my naked breasts. My hard nipples glistened with moisture. I looked down again at the pink crack of my cunt and, for a second, was seized with a desire to run my hand down and grasp its moist wet flesh. I imagined its warmth, its softness and the thrills that would run inside me as I probed my fingers into its fragrant darkness.

Two more ornate shields were brought and held on each side of me. My confusion increased. Now, amidst the clamour and frantic activity, I could see three reflections of myself!

Spitting torches burned brightly all around. I wanted desperately to blink, to lick my dry lips, to push everything away from me, to jump from the altar and run away to freedom.

Suddenly, the face of an Indian appeared in front of mine. It grinned broadly — gold teeth flashed in the flickering torchlight. A massive and complex tattooed eagle decorated his chest!

He screeched out loudly and, with his fists clenched, he held his arms upwards as if defying his gods.

There was a few seconds of silence. I could feel my heart pounding. I was filled with anxiety. I stared as the eagle on his chest seemed to move. A wave of fear spread through me. Then, as he stretched over me, the massive bird twitched. I wanted to close my eyes, shut it out, but I could not. The Indian pulled back, and I thought I saw the eagle flap its massive white-tipped wings. I wanted to shake my head, to clear it, to bring some sense back into my confused world, but still I could do nothing but stare.

The eagle flapped again, preparing itself for flight. I heard it screech. My head was filled with its terrible rasping cry. I watched its white head shaking from side it side, then it gave another ear-piercing shriek as it opened it vicious hooked beak and exposed its heavy hard tongue. It fixed me with its devilish eye — yellow with a black dot at its centre for a pupil. I saw its wings again, now opening wide, stretching the separated feathers at their tips. They both beat down powerfully at the same time. The heavy flaps echoed in my head like thunder. Slowly, the huge bird rose up, flying off the old Indian's chest, lifting its sharp yellow talons, holding them threateningly above my hard throbbing nipples.

I wanted so much to close my eyes, to blot out the terrible monster before me, but it was all I could see — I was powerless in a living, waking nightmare.

The massive bird shrieked again as it dropped down onto my breasts. It took each of my nipples in its clawing talons. Their sharp points dug in agonisingly. I wanted to shriek, to cry out, to beg, to plead for help, but my anguish was silent. Every scream I had was locked inside my unresponsive body. The razor sharp talons clawed at my nipples — digging into them, pulling at them, penetrating me with fiery tongues of piercing pain.

I began again to see the images of myself in the shields. It was as if I was someone else who was watching; as if I was detached from myself, observing myself. A face in a headdress was between my legs. I could see a long wet tongue licking at my cunt. My legs were being held wide by the knees. And I was powerless to resist. When the face lifted away it was replaced by another. This time the tongue delved into my anus. I watched its tip penetrating me, pushing into the dark ring, opening it up with its pressure then driving in as far as its length would allow.

I just stared — racked with the pain in my nipples as the eagle's talons dug in ever deeper, violated by the delving tongue in my anus, fearful of my complete inability to move, terrified of what would happen next.

I heard another shriek from the massive bird. I watched my breasts stretched by the tension on my nipples. Suddenly it released its grip and flew above me.

An Indian came forward with a tomahawk in his hand — coloured feathers dangled from the beaded handle. He offered the bulbous butt end to the slit of my cunt. I watched the soft flesh open at its touch. I saw the glistening of my own moisture on the yielding folds. He twisted it several times, opening me, exposing me, then, in one movement, he drove it in. I felt it inside me — its hardness, the ornate beadwork against my tender flesh which lined my cunt, the massive bulbous end which had looked too big to enter. I thought I felt my eyes widen but, when I looked at myself in the shields, all I could see was a passive naked victim — unresponsive, silent, violated and tortured.

He tightened his grip on the handle and thrust it as deep as it would go. I felt the bulbous end filling me, stuffing me full. I could not imagine how he had got it in and, as I felt the tugging pressure of its withdrawal, how it would come out. Another wave of fear passed through me. In the reflective shields, I watched the soft petals of flesh at the entrance to my cunt stretching around the massive end as he took it out. He held it up like a prize.

Moisture ran down the glistening shaft as it glistened in the flickering torchlight. The shields were shaken in approval and the images of myself vibrated around me while, all the time, my body remained impassive and motionless. Suddenly, he dropped the wet bulbous end against my anus and held it there. His gold teeth flashed behind his wide grinning lips.

I could do nothing but watch as he pressed it against the tight muscular ring. I saw it dilate under the pressure. He pushed the massive wet head in, held it there for a moment, and then, with a sudden thrust, drove it in deeply. I felt myself gasping, tightening, crying out, but still nothing happened — my body was totally motionless, silent, limp. I felt the carved swollen head of the handle inside — stuffing me — I felt its heavily beaded shaft against the lining of my rectum. I felt the fullness of it, but still I did not — still I could not — move.

The tip of a hot stiff cock was held across my mouth and I watched in the shields as it sprayed its semen over my face. I tasted it on my lips, smelled it in my nostrils, and saw my vision blur as it ran into my eyes, but still I lay, completely motionless, unable to respond in any way.

But, even in my enforced stillness, I felt the brewing heat inside me. My anxieties, my fear, my terror, were not enough to hold it back. He pulled the handle back. The tugging tension against the walls of my rectum and behind the distended anal ring set off a drawing sensation which ran through my whole body. My distended nipples ached, my eyes filled with tears, my cunt ran with moisture, and my clitoris pounded.

Suddenly, out of nowhere, and in a frightening flurry of beating wings, the eagle came back down on top of me. I wanted to gasp with fear but, at the same time, I wanted to welcome it, to grasp its talons and draw it down against my aching breasts. I wanted to feel its thumping wings pounding me. I wanted to rise up against it — to welcome its energy, its power.

Again it dug its sharp claws into my nipples. I yearned to cry out — to release my pain and scream out my pleasure. I wanted it to enfold me in its hammering wings. I wanted to bury myself in its muscular domination. I wanted to be engulfed by its power.

It lifted me by my nipples and, in the shimmering reflections in the shields, I saw my limp body rising up from the hard stone altar. The tomahawk was pulled from my anus and, as the last drips of semen ran down my cheeks, I was carried up into the inky sky by the terrifying bird.

I went giddy. My body, suspended by my stretched nipples, spun in the air as the eagle flew away with me as its prey.

I don't know what happened — time became stretched and then compressed. The scene changed. It was light. I was being carried above a forest. Then, far below, I saw the rushing waters of a river and the massive torrent of boiling water that flooded over a great cliff in its path.

The huge eagle held me in its yellow claws above the pounding waters of the waterfall. Its heavy flapping wings strained to keep us both in the air. Suddenly, I was falling, dropping giddily through the air, speeding dizzily towards the rushing waters of the thunderous cascade below.

The roaring water engulfed me — filling my head with noise, pounding in my ears, buffeting me from side to side. I felt I was drowning, being suffocated by the overpowering and deafening waterfall as, quickly, I was sucked down into its spiralling currents. The vortex overcame me. My eyes remained open but all I could see was the silver downpour of water in a confused turmoil around me. My limp body was tossed about by the furious storm of water. My head filled with its clamour. My mind was overcome with uncontrollable fear. I tried to swim amongst the water but it was all bubbles, there was no resistance, nothing to pull myself against. I could think only of my stuffed anus, my agonised nipples, and the flapping wings of the monstrous eagle. The crashing water tossed me about — my body was bent and twisted in the violent uproar. I realised that my attempts at swimming were imagination. Still I could not move, but it did not matter. My head was filled with desire, my body was overcome with the heat of pleasure, and the crashing waves pummelling me drove my helpless form into a sudden paroxysm of pleasure, the jerks of which were caused, not my own muscles, but by the thrashing waves and the beating foam which surrounded me.

My lips still felt numb and swollen but, as I tried to talk, I felt them quiver. My senses were coming back. Yes, I could move again! I licked my lips and felt my tongue running across them. I tasted soap. I heaved and sat forward. Yes, I could move!

'You must go. You are too wanton, too evil to take the place of the pure Telulah. Yours is surely a terrible fate. Surely you will be consumed by the thundering waters of hell. There you will fall from grace into the boiling sea of eternal sin. Turn your back on the pleasures of suffering now, or you will drown in the waters that fall from the high rocks into the boiling cauldron below.'

I could not tell where the voice was coming from.

Suddenly, I was shivering, shaking all over. Still I could not speak, but I could move. I turned my head and looked at my arms and legs.

I was saturated — foamy water ran all over me. I did not understand where I was at first, then I realised — I was in the car wash, in the back of my pick-up!

The old Indian reached out to me. His bony hand clutched mine. I pushed him off and sat upright. He reached towards me again and, still shaking, I squirmed across the drenched corrugated floor of the pick-up and slid over the wet tailgate. I shook my head, stumbled to my feet and started to make my way unsteadily around to the driver's door.

The old Indian remained sitting — silent, enigmatic, as though he had been suddenly taken by a trance. The wide brim of his hat cast a dark shade over his heavy eyes, cutting even deeper the already profound lines that laced his leathery face like the very chasms of hell. Behind him, in the sopping corner of the back of the pick-up lay a massive Indian headdress and a bead encrusted tomahawk.

Slowly he grinned — his mouth opened wide and his shining golden teeth flashed brightly. I gasped. He started taking off his shirt. I reeled back. The tattoo on his chest seemed alive. The massive bird that was emblazoned on it looked as if it could leap from his chest and carry me away in its yellow hooked talons. Yes, I was seeing it again — the great eagle. And suddenly, I realised, this old Indian must truly be the wandering Aquila, still trying to fulfil his obligation to his gods!

As I drove away, water still dripping from my hair, the taste of semen still on my lips, I realised that I had not only escaped with my life but with my soul as well.

4. Fairies in the Desert 1
BRACKEN'S STORY

I parked in the desert for most of the day — my wits were in tatters. I lay across the wide, plastic covered bench seat of the old pick-up. The sweet scent of the hot plastic filled my nostrils. I lifted my feet up and rested my heels in the open passenger window.

I had managed to grab my T shirt and jeans when I had staggered away from the old Indian, but I had lost my panties. I wriggled down lower on the seat and pushed my feet out completely through the open window. I stretched my legs, unbuttoned my jeans and slowly pulled down the zip.

It was hot and stuffy in the cab and I was sweating. I pushed my hand down the front of my stomach. Father Dawson had kept my pubic hair shaved and I felt a tingle of excitement as my fingertips glanced the smooth soft skin above my slit. I stretched them further down until my fingers reached the top of my crack. The soft flesh opened instantly, swelling and splitting into a delightful valley of silky wetness. I ran my finger into the warm slit. My clitoris was already swelling — I could feel its pulsating throb. I pressed my fingertip against it, dropped my head back and closed my eyes. I breathed in deeply as I squeezed my fingers around its throbbing base.

I licked my lips and was refreshed by their coolness as my saliva dried. Images of my captivity in Dawson's Rise came back into my mind. I saw myself again, held on the leash, the collar tight around my neck, with Father Dawson leading me from my kennel to the post for daily punishment. I felt again the slap of his flattened hand and the cut of his belt as he brought it down across my upturned buttocks. I saw myself cowering before him and I was filled again with the delightful feeling of humiliation and shame.

I felt a trickle of spit running from the corner of my mouth. I lifted my head and ran my other hand down past the first until my finger tip pressed against my anus. I felt its involuntary dilation. I allowed it to open enough to take my fingertip and, as soon as it entered, I drove it in deeply. I squeezed my fingers around my clitoris and my whole body was filled immediately with a burning and irresistible heat of desire.

I lifted my hips and looked down at my naked crack. Wetness surrounded it, my fingers glistened. I lifted it higher — I wanted to see it clearly. I wanted to reach forward and lick it. I wanted to slip my tongue into it. I wanted to feel the probing warmth of its soft wetness. I squeezed my buttocks tightly together and pressed my finger even deeper into my pulsating anus. I gasped. It was suddenly upon me. I had no time to revel in it, no time to enjoy the build-up of excitement. I could not hold back the overpowering tide of joy — it surged through me in an abrupt and unstoppable gush.

My head spun giddily. My body shook. A sudden jolt made me twist. A torrent of noise ran through my ears. I was filled with a tension so powerful I felt I would explode. I took another sharp intake of breath. There was a momentary pause, everything went silent — a moment of expectation — then, from nowhere there was a bang, a heavy loud bang deep inside my head. It echoed down into my fingertips, overpowered me and sent me into an unexpected yelping seizure. My body contorted with an uncontrollable paroxysm. I drove my fingers tightly inside my cunt. I felt its quivering sloppiness. I held onto my flesh — gripping it, hanging onto it, as if releasing my hold on it would release me from my grip on life itself. I buried my finger deeply into my anus and forced myself down onto it as hard as I could. My mouth fell wide open and I heard my own unnatural scream — it was as though my fractured soul was releasing itself from my body.

I lifted my head forward, dropped my mouth wide and started choking as my throat tightened and spit flowed uncontrollably over my tongue. Spit splattered from my mouth and I yelled out loud, not words — nothing that was coherent — just a long yell, something to use my bursting breath on, something to let out the life-seizing tension which threatened to overtake me completely from within.

Suddenly, I heard something. I held my breath and did not move. I listened. There it was again — a child-like giggle. I looked up and froze.

A girl was peering in through the window. When she caught my eye, she held her hand to her mouth to disguise her giggling. Her eyes were bright and wide, her dark hair was cut short, and, on her shoulders she wore a pair of delicate pink fairy wings.

I drew my feet back into the pick-up and, trembling all over, looked around to find my jeans — I did not even remember taking them off.

'It's okay,' said the fairy girl. 'I like to look. I have been watching ever since you started. You were very noisy. Very noisy! But it's okay, most people are.'

I felt embarrassed by her openness and ashamed that she had seen what I had been doing without my knowing.

She smiled broadly, her white teeth flashed in the sunlight.

'I do that all the time. If it wasn't for that, I'd go crazy in this place. Can I get in with you? We can do it together if you like.'

I was taken aback by her forthrightness.

She opened the door. I pulled my legs up and she sat on the edge of the seat. Her delicate wings pressed against the door pillar. She was the picture of beauty. Her pink wings were fixed tightly to her delightful bare shoulders with a delicately made shoulder harness. Around their edges dark mauve lines were traced in lacy scribbles. Attached somehow to the base of the wings were two curled antennae which sprang up and down as she moved. A powdery gathering of fluffy white feathers were placed where the two wings joined together. Around her neck she had a fluffy heart shaped necklace and on each wrist a matching fluffy band.

'My name's Bracken Rainbowflower. I'm so happy to meet you.'

She reached in, shook my hand and kept hold of it. Her hand was not too warm, nor too cold — it was the perfect temperature.

She was a fantastic apparition — a fairy in the desert! I could hardly believe what I was seeing.

'Come with me. Meet the others.'

She smiled broadly and tugged at my hand.

She wore a filmy lilac and purple skirt with a lightly embroidered low cut bodice to match. Her breasts were small but her nipples were hard and prominent. As she pulled at me she opened her legs for purchase against the pick-up seat and, for a moment, I saw her pink panties pulled tightly against the flesh of her slit. I wanted to press the insides of her knees and open her legs. I wanted to pull her satiny panties down so that I could lick her naked crack, taste it, and inhale its mouth-watering fragrance. I wanted to lap at it, drink from its delectable spring of sweetness.

'Come on!' she insisted. 'Come on!'

She dragged me out of the pick-up. She was irresistible.

Suddenly, outside the pick-up I felt the blistering heat of the sun. I held my spare hand up to my forehead to shade my eyes.

'Come on! Come on!' she kept shouting excitedly.

She pulled me through a barely open panel in a security fence.

The first thing I saw was the tower — a metal framework perhaps fifty feet high rising from the scrubby desert which surrounded it.

'That's the tower. Oh, I do love flying!' she shouted. 'And look! There's everyone waiting to meet you. What's your name? Tell me your name so that I can introduce you properly.'

'Syra,' I said as she pulled me in amongst a group clustered around a loose tangle of old motorhomes and caravans decorated with graffiti and psychedelia.

Chattering young women gathered around me. Like Bracken they were dressed in diaphanous skirts, bodices and wings. One was green, one blue, one was made up like a butterfly with antennae in her hair, one had wings of feathers, one had silver hair and wings, and one was painted all over in gold with curling antennae sprouting from her hair. They buzzed around me, repeating my name, touching my hair, my face, and my breasts.

As they settled, each one curtsied and introduced themselves in turn.

The all had strange names — Field Goblinwind, Feather Saturnwitch, Fidget Goblinfly, Field Elffrost,

Bramble Elffrost, Fidget Goblinfilter. When they had introduced themselves, they made me sit on a cushion in their midst. They flocked around me, holding my hands, touching me and repeating their names. One pushed her face up close to mine and began kissing me. Her lips were soft and sweet. She probed her long tongue into my mouth. She licked around my own tongue and the insides of my cheeks. I felt its tip touching the back of my throat. Suddenly she broke away and fell back in front of me, giggling and writhing on the ground. Her green wings crumpled behind her delightfully square bare shoulders and her legs came up to reveal her light green panties pulled tightly against her cunt. I could just make out the shadow of darker green that ran along the crack of her tight slit. She was a delicious sight.

'That's Field Goblinwind,' said Bracken. 'She can be very silly sometimes. She always wants to do things too soon. She can be so naughty. Here, follow me. You must have some refreshment. Here. Come into my bower.'

She pulled me into the back of an old VW camper. It was filled with flowers and lacy shreds of material that hung from the brightly decorated roof.

She sat beside me on a red cushioned seat.

'Do you like my little nest? We each have one. Sir Orfeo visits us in turn but, of course, we do his bidding continually. Can I kiss you? You are so beautiful. Can I?'

She drew closer to me and draped her hands around my neck. She looked up into my eyes and poked out her tongue.

'See? Would you like me to put my tongue inside your mouth? Would you?'

She leant across me and licked at my face. Her tongue

was wet and soft. She lapped at my cheeks and my eyes. She ran the tip of her tongue into my ears, wetting them, probing them. I felt myself pushing against her, wanting her to do more. She licked at my lips and opened them so that her tongue could go in. Its probing tip searched around the insides of my lips, licking in the spit that was there then, suddenly she pulled back.

'Or I could lick there!'

She pushed the flat of her hand between my thighs and pressed it against my cunt.

'But you must be dressed like us. You must be a fairy too! Yes, you can be the fairy Syra. Perhaps Sir Orfeo will christen you properly. Here, lift up your arms. You must be naked to start.'

I had not even realised that I had left my jeans in the pick-up. I felt a flush of embarrassment come over my face.

'Oh, you're embarrassed. Perhaps the mention of Sir Orfeo's name. Yes, that's what it is. It happens to me sometimes.'

She held my hands and kissed me firmly on the lips. I felt the flesh of my naked cunt swelling with desire.

'It's so exciting to have someone new!'

She poked about inside the old van pulling out different pieces of material, feathers and wings. At last she decided on something and held up a tight, light green bodice. She laughed at my erect nipples and sucked at them for a while, and bit them softly, before she resigned herself to cover them.

'Your nipples are very sweet!' she said excitedly as she pulled back.

She gave me a thin green skirt which clipped at the back of my waist. It was short, hardly coming halfway down my thighs.

She held up a pair of light green satin panties.

'And these! But I must lick you before you put them on. Here, let me kneel between your legs. Open your knees. Oh, your cunt is so beautiful — so pink and neat.'

She lowered her face between my thighs and laid the flat of her tongue across the flesh of my cunt. It was wet already, but I felt it open against the light pressure of her soft tongue. Then I felt the tip of her tongue probing around my clitoris. She pressed it against the base, licked it as it hardened, sucked at it as it extended. Then I felt her tongue inside, licking at the soft flesh within, pressing against the outer edges, spreading her delicate spit across them, sucking at my own moisture, nourishing herself like a butterfly at a flower.

I leant back against the inside of the old van. I stared at the bunches of multicoloured flowers which hung from the ribbons stretched across the inside of the roof. I opened my legs as wide as I could. I looked down at her, this fragile fairy, her face buried in the flesh of my cunt, her eyes, just occasionally looking up at me, checking I was still there, as if in her delectable reverie she might lose track of everything in the world, even the object of her angelic passion.

Her pert nose glistened — covered with the moisture from my cunt — as she ran it up the valley of flesh. She lapped so keenly at its centre, letting the tip of her tongue first run in then curl around the base of my throbbing clitoris. She pressed her hands against the insides of my thighs, widening them with the slightest pressure — gently opening me with her own sweet delicacy. The antennae on her wings bobbed up and down, springing open and closed and her wings rose and fell. It was as if they were flapping in preparation for her to take to the air. I was hypnotised by her loveliness.

A tingling heat began to grow inside me. I rose higher and pressed harder — I wanted her tongue as deep as she could get it, I wanted her to drink from my cunt, suck the nectar from it, and nourish herself with its honey.

She looked up at me, her eyes bright and clear — she was magnetic. I groaned as I took each of my nipples between a thumb and forefinger and squeezed as hard as I could. The pain burned into me, raced through my veins and joined the scorching joy that was flowing from my cunt. Then I cried out as, suddenly, without any further warning, I went rigid with a sharp and brutal orgasm.

Bracken looked up and smiled. She wriggled up between my legs and lay on my chest. I was panting and trembling.

'Would you like to hear my story? About how I came to be here? Oh yes, I must tell you. Oh Syra, dear Syra. Your cunt is so sweet. I love the taste of it. Have I licked it enough? Did I get the tip of my tongue in deep enough? Here, let me kiss you so that you can taste it as well.'

She pulled herself up and kissed me. Her soft full lips opened against mine and her tongue entered my mouth. I could taste my cunt and, as her taut body squirmed on top of me, and she kissed me keenly, I felt another shuddering orgasm gripping me like a vice.

'There,' she said. 'Now, how did I get here? Well it started at a party. It was fancy dress. I was there as a fairy. It was my first time. Sir Orfeo was there as a demon — he was only called 'Orfeo' then. He took to me a bedroom and said he wanted to spank me — he said he thought my bottom was delightful. I had never been spanked before, well, you know, not "properly". He told me not to take anything off but just to bend over the edge of the bed. I didn't know what to expect, but I did exactly as he said. He looked at me for quite a while, walking around, inspecting me I suppose. Then he rubbed his hand across the surface of my panties — I remember them so well, they were light mauve, satin, tight, and they covered my buttocks completely. Yes, he smoothed his hand across them — it felt delightful. There was something about the satiny surface that added to the sensation of his touch — it was so smooth, so sheer, so exquisite. And the material moved ever so slightly over the surface of my bottom as he stroked it. Then he peeled them down, slowly, very slowly. He held the waistband and pulled it away from my skin then drew the material down bit by bit. I felt the coolness of the air as my skin was exposed to it. I was so excited. Slowly, they came down until the waistband was just beneath the notch at the base of my bottom — where my bottom joins the tops of my thighs. He let it go and I felt the sudden snapping pressure of it — I moaned, I remember that, I moaned. Then he stood back and looked at me again. I didn't know if I should do something — open my buttocks, or tighten them. I did nothing. Then he stood sideways and held his hand back at full stretch. I could just see a reflection of him in a mirror. I waited, I don't know how long — seconds, minutes, I couldn't tell. Then I saw in the mirror his hand coming down, then I heard the smack, then I felt the jolt, then I felt the sting, then I cried out, then I had an orgasm. Just like that. One smack.

'I squeezed my eyes shut every time his hand came down, but I opened them again as soon as I could to see him in the mirror. I don't know how many he gave me. All I know is that I cried and that he gave me a handkerchief to wipe my eyes and blow my nose. He told me to pull my panties up and sit on the edge of the bed and wait. He left and came back a few minutes later with an older man. They talked for a while then Sir Orfeo told me to bend over the bed as I had done before. I did what I was told. I never thought to do otherwise. I watched this man in the mirror as well. But I was still sore, and this man was more vicious, his hand was rough and each time he smacked me I was knocked forward hard against the edge of the bed. Once I tried to get up but Sir Orfeo pushed me back down and the man continued. I cried a lot after he had done with me. Sir Orfeo said he would take me back to his flat and I could have a bath. I went with him and that night I cried myself to sleep in a strange bed with a strange man.

'The next day he bought me some new fairy clothes — much finer, more satiny, and the panties fitted my bottom better, like the one's I have on now. That night he took me out again to another party. This time he paraded me in front of everyone else as soon as we arrived. He made me prance and skip and had me jump off the edge of a sofa as if I was flying. He called me his own "little fairy" and asked if anyone wanted to spank me, particularly, he said, if they thought I done something naughty. One man said that he thought my wings were not straight enough and that was a good reason for a spanking. They all laughed and I was made to bend over there and then so that the man could spank me. After that others found more reasons and so, in a short while, my bottom was red and sore and tears filled my eyes. Then I was spanked for crying and then for not crying enough.

'From then on, I was made to do more things. Sir Orfeo showed me how to suck cocks, how to take them deeply into my throat and how to swallow the semen without taking them out. Sometimes I was allowed to lick cunts, but not as much as I wanted. Once he found me licking a woman's cunt and he was so angry he thrashed me with a cane. The next day he showed me his wand, a cane he had made and decorated with stars. He said it would work magic on me. He thrashed me with it there and then, to show me, he said, what would happen if I ever thought of disobeying him.

'One night, one of the men Sir Orfeo was showing me off to, said he had never seen me fly, and I couldn't be a fairy if I couldn't fly. Sir Orfeo wrapped a rope around my chest and dangled me from the balcony. They all laughed and shouted at me, struggling fearfully as I hung suspended over the street below.

'At one party he picked up another girl. It was nice to have a friend. Soon there were several of us. He christened us with fairy names. In the mornings he instructed us on sexual practice — how to do things and also how to bear the pain that the tormentors he allowed to use us provided. In the evenings we were taken out to clubs and parties, sometimes as a group, sometimes alone or in pairs or threes.

'Then, one day, he announced that we were all leaving and going to the desert. He had bought several old vehicles and we drove here to find that, behind a heavy wired security fence, he had already built his 'flying machine'. The machine, he said which would prove we were all true fairies.

'We were all trained on the machine and clients started to come from miles around to watch us and then use us as they wished. Oh Syra, it is so good to lick your cunt. Will you lick mine? Sir Orfeo won't allow that any more.

Will you, Syra? Will you? Please, Syra, will you lick my cunt?'

Bracken draped her legs over my shoulders as I knelt before her. She had taken her panties off quickly, throwing them on the floor of the old van before lying back on the seat and asking me to start.

Her cunt was so sweet — wet, scented, and fragrant. The flesh was soft and pliable and the slit at its centre was pink and glistening with moisture. As I laid my tongue against it, she lifted her hips and cried out. It was a soft moaning cry, like a song. Yes, it was as if she was singing. I sensed her joy and, I don't know how, I also sensed that this pleasure was more than she was allowed by her master, Sir Orfeo.

5. Fairies in the Desert 2
THE FLYING MACHINE

Suddenly, the side doors of the van burst open.

'Bracken!' shouted a man's voice. 'Out!'

Bracken pulled back. I felt a cool draft of air against my wet face.

'Sir Orfeo!' she cried out, dropping to her knees before him. 'I know I have done wrong. I only went outside the fence to pick some desert flowers. Last night there was a shower of rain, and they are so beautiful. Punish me, please punish me. Oh, it was so wrong of me. But, Sir, her cunt is so sweet, it is like nectar, and you know I must feed. And it was only right to let her feed from me.'

He placed both his hands on her head.

'Yes, I will punish you. Do not fret, my child. Your bottom will not escape my hand.' Bracken furrowed her brow and scowled — she was clearly disappointed. 'Or… my wand.'

Her face suddenly lit up and she beamed widely in excited approval.

'Yes! Yes! Your wand!'

She looked up at him intently.

Sir Orfeo was tall. His dark hair was held together in a long pony tail by a trailing purple ribbon. His face was angular and tanned. His eyes were bright blue and glittered in the dazzling sunlight. He wore a purple smock which reached the ground. His voice was soft and low. In his hand he held a black wand with tiny sparkling stars painted along its full tapering length.

'And who is this beauty? Who dresses as one of my little fairy band but is unknown to me?' He looked down disapprovingly at the still kneeling Bracken. 'Who is it that has led my little Bracken astray?'

'She is Syra,' urged Bracken. 'And her cunt is as sweet as apple blossom honey.'

'Be silent!' he shouted to her. 'Your chattering is too much. Line up with the others. Your bottom needs to feel my wand sooner than I thought.'

Bracken jumped up and ran in amongst the others. They squabbled over places but, with some elbowing and pushing, they slowly brought themselves into a line.

'Come, Syra. You can see my little band of fairies. See how obedient they are. See how they rush to obey every command I give them. Come.'

He opened his hand and let me walk ahead of him towards Bracken and the others. The green panties I had on were tight and pulled up between the crease of my buttocks. He lifted the hem of my short dress to look. I felt a wave of excitement surge between my buttocks. I hoped he would bend me over and look closer, or tell me to run into the line next to Bracken so that I could bend for his admonishing wand.

'See how excited they are at the thought of taking my wand across their tight little bottoms. Follow me, Syra. Watch carefully and maybe you will be given a chance to earn your own wings.'

I followed him as he approached the line of excited fairies. Their wings sparkled in the bright sunlight, their antennae bobbed, and those that had headdresses nodded like butterflies sipping from a refreshing mountain spring. Bracken was at the far end of the line. She leant forward and smiled to me. I smiled back and she gave me a hurried wave with a hand she lifted only quickly and then only to shoulder height. She bobbed back quickly as Sir Orfeo stood at the other end.

'You see we have a visitor, my little angels. Her name is Syra — if you have not already found out.'

They all giggled and leant forward to look.

'Perhaps Syra might want to join you. We must show her our little ways, show her the pleasures that we take part in.'

They all nodded excitedly.

'Please! Please! Please!'

Sir Orfeo Laughed.

'Turn around , my little fairies. Show Syra your best behaviour, and your best obedience.'

Still in line, they turned around.

One of them bent forward and lifted her short skirt. Her shiny silver panties caught the light, and the tight cleft at the centre of the gusset darkened in the sudden shadow.

'Field Goblinwind!' shouted Sir Orfeo. 'You are too eager. Stand up until I tell you! Stand upright. Until you are instructed to do otherwise, stand upright!'

She pulled her dress down and, shaking her wings in a shiver of frustration, she stood up with her arms rigidly by her sides.

Bracken leant around and smiled at me as if to say 'I told you so.'

'Now, my fairies, lift the hems of your skirts. But slowly! I want to see your panties uncovered bit by bit, not all at once. I want to see how tight your bottoms are, how closely the material covers them. I want to see the cleft between your buttocks and how much the material of your panties is pulled into it. Slowly, my little angels. You will all have your fair share.'

Together they took hold of the hems of their short diaphanous skirts and lifted them enough to expose their panties. Each wore a different colour — silver, green, mauve, pink, gold, turquoise and opal white. Bracken ran her finger along the tight leg of her panties as she lifted her skirt, pulling it upwards and showing more of the taut cheeks of her buttocks on either side of the tight crack between them than would have been visible without her assistance. Again, she leant out of the line and smiled to me. She opened her eyes wide, dipped her head and squeezed up her shoulders. She was delectable.

Sir Orfeo saw her this time and walked over to her angrily.

'Bracken! I tire of your disobedience! Come here!'

Bracken ran over excitedly. She bent before him and lifted her skirt. She had not pulled up her panties completely.

'Pull your panties down and wait here. I will attend to you later.'

She smiled at me under her eyelashes. She looked as if she was barely able to contain her excitement, or perhaps she held a secret that was too much to keep. I could see her excitement was boiling over.

She remained, bending over, her panties down — a delectable fawn — the antennae fixed to her back bobbing and sparkling in the desert sunlight.

She peeped out of the line again and widened her eyes precociously. This time Sir Orfeo saw her. He was enraged. He ran forward along the line of fairies. He brought his wand down cuttingly across her bare buttocks. She yelped loudly. He brought it down again. She fell forward. He turned to the others — many of them were giggling and holding their hands to their mouths.

He kicked at Bracken as she struggled to get to her feet. She wrapped her arms around his legs. He tried to shake her off but she would not let go. He dragged her along roughly.

'Pull your panties down!' he shouted angrily to the others. 'Pull them down to your knees!'

Field Goblinwind was the first to feel the lashing contact of his wand. It came down so viciously — it contained all his anger. She did not yell out — it was as if the cutting slash was too painful. Her head dropped slightly and heavy silent tears fell from her eyes.

I winced each time the wand came down and my own body tightened with fear as I saw the red lines that quickly spread across her tight, pale skinned buttocks.

As she was slowly overcome by the pain, her body relaxed and her buttocks widened. But Sir Orfeo's wand did not relent. Its sharp edge cut against the exposed oval of her cunt, marking lines across the soft pinkness of her delectable flesh.

Suddenly, as if seized by a fresh thought, and still with Bracken hanging onto his legs, he marched to Bramble Elffrost. She gritted her teeth, knowing what would happen, knowing that now, punishment could not be avoided. He kicked at Bracken but still she clung on. Her tenaciousness only increased his frustration. He ran his fingers between the cheeks of Bramble Elffrost's buttocks. She tightened them. He pinched her hard. She flinched and it angered him even more.

Bramble cried loudly as the wand came down. She sobbed as it continued and, the more she showed her suffering, the harder he beat her, and, the harder he beat her, the more improbable it seemed that he would stop.

I watched as, in turn, all the others took the same beating — each one knowing what had preceded her own punishment, each one knowing that hers would be worse.

Some of them dropped to their knees, Bramble and Field Goblinwind stayed standing. They all cried. As Sir Orfeo finished punishing the last one in the line, he bent over and started thrashing Bracken who still held on tightly to his legs. She clung on as long as she could but, in the end, her grip loosened and she let go. She lay curled up on the floor as he continued beating her. In the end, he pulled her to her feet and made her stand, still bent over and still with her panties pulled down to her knees.

At last it seemed as if he had slaked his thirst for inflicting pain and he marched the rest of them in a line to the tower at the centre of the compound. It was a latticed rigging of ironwork about fifty feet to the top. Its base was fixed onto a heavy crane platform with outriggers leading to massive steel stabilising pads. A huge diesel engine was fixed to the base and a mess of cogs, shafts and wheels led to a flat steel wheel upon which the tower itself was mounted. At its top there was a circular platform and from the platform dangled several heavy ropes.

'This is my flying machine,' Sir Orfeo said proudly. He stalked around its heavy base. 'I invented it myself. It is where my little fairies get their wings. Only if they show they can fly on my machine can they earn them. Look how they prance at its feet. See how their excitement overwhelms them.'

All the fairies ran around the huge metal feet splayed out from the heavy base which anchored the tower and held it fast to the massive engine beneath.

'Come, my little flock, help Syra. She needs to feel the elation of my wonderful machine. And perhaps she will learn the art of flight. She could earn her wings and then perhaps she will be able to join you, another member of my beautiful band of fairies.'

I looked back to Bracken. She had not moved. A sudden whirl of wind blew across the desert scrub. It picked up a spiral of dust and drove a ball of sage brush ahead. The wind lifted the hem of her lilac and purple skirt and her delicate pink wings fluttered in its draught. Then, suddenly, as she gave me one last flashing capricious glance, the twisting shroud of dust enveloped her in its cloaking corkscrew.

The others pulled at me and led me up some metal steps to the base of the flying machine. They made me stand with my back to the tower. Sir Orfeo started the massive engine. The heavy vibrations came up through my feet. I felt them running into my face — my lips trembled, my eyes blinked.

He dropped a lever forward and I heard gears grinding behind me. He reached up and took one of the ropes which dangled from the platform at the top of the tower.

'Now we shall see if you can earn your wings.'

He held up a harness with green wings in front of me.

'These are training wings,' he said. 'Barely enough to keep you aloft, but enough to see if you deserve a proper pair.'

He laughed and pulled the harness around my shoulders.

He wound a strap around my ankles and clipped the end of the rope into it with a karabiner. He tugged at it and I fell forward. He laughed again. It was as though he was tormenting me — as though he had already decided I would fail. He led the rope up between my shoulder blades and clipped it twice into the harness somewhere between the two small wings.

The fairy girls fussed around me, touching my face, my breasts, my cunt. Field Goblinwind started kissing me. She probed her tongue into my mouth. I could not resist. There was a deep sense of excitement inside me — the exposure, the fear, the control of Sir Orfeo, was conspiring to brew up a storm of joy within me against which I was unable to stand.

I started to suck at Field Goblinwind's tongue. She pushed her hand down between the tops of my thighs and ran her finger into the panty-covered crack of my cunt. I breathed in deeply as her tongue went deeper and her fingertips pressed harder. I felt other hands on my breasts — pinching my nipples, pulling them, squeezing them painfully. I sucked harder on Field Goblinwind's tongue. Her spit ran into my mouth. I drank it down — it was cool and foamy, sweet and delectable.

Suddenly the massive engine revved and I felt a yank on my back. I fell forwards. Field Goblinwind and the others pulled away. I was left gaping, spit running over my bottom lip, my eyes wide with fear, my hands reaching forward in a hopeless attempt to save myself.

A wave of fear ran through me as, struggling to keep my balance, I was hauled up on the rope. The attachments were balanced so that I was held on the harness, lying horizontally in the air. I spun as the rope was pulled up then, as suddenly as it had started to haul me up, it stopped. The rope jolted. I thought I would fall. I spun faster as the fairies below ran around in an excited bunch, pointing up at me, prancing, giggling, and kissing each other.

A cloud of black smoke blew up from the massive engine below as Sir Orfeo revved it and threw another heavy control lever. I choked as the smoke engulfed me. I sensed movement and realised that the tower was turning. I looked down and saw that I was being taken around in an increasingly fast circle as the tower turned and I was lifted further from the ground as I was thrown outwards on the rope by the centrifugal force it imparted.

I was still spinning on the rope but now I was also circling the tower on the rope which, as it speeded up, was flinging me out into an ever wider circle. I was terrified. My heart was pounding. I was shaking all over. I felt the little wings on my back vibrating and flapping as I went faster and faster. I stared down to the ground below. The fairies looked minute as they ran around the tower trying to keep up with me as I was flung in a massive circle above them. For a moment, it felt as though I was really flying. I saw the full circle of the perimeter fence around the compound of motorhomes and caravans. Then something started to judder. My harness was loose!

The force of being flung outwards on the rope made my hands and feet feel heavy. I couldn't keep my mouth closed. The harness was shaking at my back. I couldn't move. I couldn't scream out for help. There was a jolt. I twisted on the rope. It felt as if one of the karabiners had come undone. I saw the fairies below pointing up. I think I heard them screaming and shouting. I saw a figure crouched at the perimeter fence. It was Bracken. Her pink wings and lilac and purple skirt were picked out by the blazing sun. Another jolt. I tried to scream but did not know whether I made any sound. I was twisted sideways and was flung upside down.

I saw Sir Orfeo running towards the base of the tower. My head was spinning. I felt nauseous. He struggled with the levers of the engine. Another cloud of black smoke rose up and engulfed me. I coughed and choked. I heard the engine revving, clattering, banging. Shudders came through the rope. My wide eyes were ablaze with fear. Light and dark flashed in front of me as I hung precariously on the rope — the blaze of the sun then nothing except black smoke.

The smoke cleared but then I hardly dared to look down. When I did, all I could see was Sir Orfeo climbing up the tower. He waved to me and shouted something, but I did not hear what he said — I was too confused and frightened.

The rotation eventually slowed and gradually I was let down until I hung close to the tower. Finally, Sir Orfeo reached out and grabbed me. He pulled me up against the tower and immediately turned me around so that he could inspect the harness.

I clung to the tower, shaking all over. Sir Orfeo muttered something, threw down one of the karabiners and struggled with the other. It was obvious something had gone wrong.

'Who has tampered with this?' he shouted down. 'Who has tampered with this harness? I will thrash you all until the culprit confesses. Who was it?'

I looked down. I couldn't see anyone. The compound was empty — all the fairies had gone.

'Who was it?' he shouted vainly as he clung to the tower and shook his fist with unbridled rage.

He left me hanging there, swinging on the rope throughout the cold, starry night. My arms and legs hung down limply. My shoulders ached with the strain of my body weight suspended on the tightly fixed harness. It did not take me long to realise that I had been duped. I knew now that Bracken and the others had deceived me — their only aim was to escape from their cruel master and they had used me as a distraction. Perhaps it was Bracken who had tampered with the harness. The excited gleam I had seen in her eyes now made perfect sense. I could not imagine where they had gone. The last I saw of them was the merest shimmer of their wings as they ran into the scrubby desert which surrounded Sir Orfeo's encampment.

When the sun came up with its welcome warmth, Sir Orfeo drove off in a pick-up. I thought I had been abandoned but, when a few hours later he returned, I realised he had tried to find them and had failed. I looked down on him and watched his angry tantrums — kicking over tables, throwing the fairies' clothes from the backs of caravans and mobile homes, sloshing petrol over them and setting them alight with an explosive blast of fire. He sat around the blaze as it sent up a curling plume of black smoke into the blue cloudless sky. Then, he turned and looked up at me. I saw the anger in his eyes, and I could see he blamed me — if I had never turned up then his obedient band of beautiful fairies may never have had the opportunity to run from him. Yes, I could see he blamed me and that he intended to punish me for what had befallen him.

He started the huge engine that drove the flying machine and lowered me down to the ground. The rope jolted and jerked as I descended. I stood up but stumbled — dizzy and suddenly confused by the feel of solid earth beneath my feet.

He grabbed my hair and dragged me to the small square where he had beaten the fairies so brutally.

'Now, you will take your turn, but do not expect to get away with a light thrashing, like my treacherous little fairies. No, you will feel the full force of my wand. Soon you will be begging me to winch you back up onto the flying machine so that your flesh need not suffer the agony of its kiss. Yes, now you will feel the pain that my little traitors would have felt if I had captured them and brought them back to their rightful home. Yes, Syra, you will feel not only the pain of your own punishment, but the pain of punishment due to all those you have helped escape.'

He made me stand and bend over. He lifted the hem of my skirt. I felt giddy with my head hanging down, but I braced my hands on my knees and hoped I would not fall and make him even angrier.

To start with he rubbed his hand across the tight material of my light green satin panties, but I could tell he would not be able to hold back his angry frustration for long. Suddenly, he ripped them down

They tore at the flesh of my cunt, pulling at it more as I curled over to try and stop the pain. He yanked them again and brought them down to my knees. My cunt throbbed with pain. He grabbed my hips and made me stand upright again. I felt the trickle of tears coming from the corners of my eyes.

He smoothed his hand across my naked buttocks, feeling their tautness and the tightness of the fissure between them. I knew he could see my cunt — its fleshy oval squeezed tight between the tops of my thighs. He ran his finger between my buttocks and into the fleshy gutter of my slit. He pressed his fingertip against it and I felt it yield and open against the pressure. His hand came away. I took a deep breath and, as a strange, almost mystical silence arose all around me, I waited for the certainty of pain.

The silence lasted for only a second. Suddenly, I fell forward against my bracing hands on my knees as the palm of his hand smacked down on my waiting bottom. I gasped in shock then cried out in pain. Then the next came down, and the next, until I was gasping and crying out in a terrible rhythm that followed the waves of stinging agony imparted by his hand. Once I began to fall forwards and he stopped, wrapped his hand around my waist and bringing me back upright. He struck each of my buttocks, sometimes in turn, sometimes smacking each one several times before he changed to the next. I felt their burning redness as the fire of pain he inflicted rose throughout my body in a blaze of pain — I was alight with a fire of pleasure.

Then, as quickly as it had started, it stopped. I began panting, getting my breath back, feeling relieved that it was all over and that I had stood it without further admonishment for disobedience or failure. I licked at my dry lips and almost turned to face him, imagining him smiling and telling me it was all over, but I was so wrong.

I heard the swish of his wand before it struck, but only for a fraction of a second. I knew what it was when I heard it, and I started to brace myself, but it came too quickly for my body to carry out the instruction from my brain.

It cut across my already stinging bottom like a burning knife. I howled in pain. The sting went so deep. It penetrated every part of my body — radiating out from my bottom, through my cunt into my nipples, and then ran into my fingertips and toes. I felt my hands trembling as I clung to my knees in a desperation to withstand it.

Then another, this time harder, slashed against my taut upturned buttocks. My mouth was wide open. I did not even hear my scream — I just saw the spray of spit flying from my mouth.

I don't know how long it lasted. I didn't know how I managed to stand, to hold onto my knees, to keep my naked bottom available to the thrashing with the wand. The cutting slices blurred into one, punctuated only by the agonising flashes of excruciating pain that shot through me as the wand struck the flesh of my squeezed out cunt.

I watched tears dripping from my eyes, and between their droplets, the spiral of spit as it dribbled from my moaning mouth. When he did stop I did not move. I did not know whether I would have to suffer more, or if I was able to move anyway. I barely felt his hands splaying my thighs wide as he opened my cunt enough to thrust his massive throbbing cock into the burning wet flesh of my crack.

He rode me with his cock — his hands around my waist, his teeth biting my ears in turn, his hot breath burning my neck. He plugged my mouth with his fingers and pulled at my hair as he held me off the ground and thrust me in a fit of anger and vengeance. In the end, he forced me down against his throbbing shaft as his semen filled me in a massive hot deluge.

He left me on the ground, his semen still bubbling from my cunt, as again he drove off into the desert in search of his lost band of beautiful fairies.

I dragged myself up and drove on the opposite direction. I looked in the rear view mirror and watched the steel gantry of the flying machine slowly disappearing over the scrubby desert horizon behind me. Only when it had completely fallen from view did I dare stop, have a drink and pull on my panties.

6. NEVADA
MAIZIE'S RANCH

At last, there it was. At the end of the dusty dirt track road, a tangle of low flat-roofed buildings, decked with gaudy neon signs and surrounded by a jumble of randomly parked SUVs and pick-ups. Yes, there it was, exactly as the picture in the magazine had showed it — 'Maizie's Ranch — the friendliest whorehouse in Nevada'.

I thought it would be an easy way to earn some money. I needed it, I had hardly enough to fill the pick-up with gas, and over the last few days it had developed a noisy clonk in the engine. I couldn't afford to let anything go wrong with it — I still had to put some distance between me and Father Dawson, and, as yet, the miles I had driven were nowhere enough.

'Just do what you're told and you'll make enough dough in a week to keep you going for a month,' said Maizie, as she introduced me to some of the other girls. 'And if you offer "specials", well, all the better.'

'That sounds interesting —"specials"?'

'"Interesting" is one way of describing it. "Weird" is another.'

A tingle of excitement ran across my skin. I felt my nipples harden.

'What do you mean "weird"?' I asked, as I took a deep breath.

'They don't come any weirder than the men who come to Maizie's Ranch, my dear. That's what they expect — and that's what they get. Here, I'll show you around.'

The building was a maze of rooms and corridors. Red lights hung in clusters from the ceilings. Each room had a name on the door: 'Kristal', 'Brooke', 'Dahlia', 'Lexy'. There were several jacuzzis, a small gymnasium, an office and a mixture of lounges.

Maizie opened the door to a room marked 'Waiting Room 1'. A young girl in a black suit with a white shirt and dark tie stood at the door. Her hands were folded across her crotch. Her skin was perfect. She smiled as we entered.

'This is where they choose the girls,' said Maizie. 'But they have to negotiate with each one to agree their menu.'

'Menu?'

'What they want. All the standard stuff is written down — breast massage, hot oils, different liquids in their mouths for cock sucking, bondage, blindfolds. They just choose and agree the price. But the weird stuff — well, that's different. Here sit down. You can watch what happens.'

'I flopped down on a massive red sofa. Several men lounged on chairs around me. Some of them sipped beers, some played nervously with their fingers. One looked at me. I could see the shape of his hard cock squeezed against the material of his trousers. He rubbed his hand across it and grinned.

A curtain was pulled aside and a line of beautiful young women strode in. They stood in a row in front of us. Two had on short skirts — one dark blue and tightly pleated, the other a white tennis skirt loosely clipped with a large safety pin. The first wore a shirt and tie, the second matched her tennis skirt with a complementary sports top. The third wore a long slinky red evening dress the cut of which closely followed her curvaceous body. The fourth one was in a tightly fitted, shiny mauve, one piece bathing suit.

She was the last to enter and stepped forward first. She tossed back her long blonde hair and moistened her full, red glossed lips with the tip of her glistening pink tongue.

'My name's Kristal. I like swimming and all water sports. Sometimes I keep on my costume. Sometimes I like to do things in the nude. I'm keen to talk about specials, and sometimes I don't even charge extra.'

She ran her right hand down the tight cleavage of her ample breasts. She stretched her fingers down into the well defined crack of her fleshy cunt beneath the tight material of the swimming suit. She smiled broadly, exposed her large white teeth, and stepped back into the line.

The girl in the tennis skirt stepped forward.

As she moved, her short white skirt opened. The large safety pin was fixed too high to keep it closed — almost on her hip. Her long, tanned, athletic thighs were fully exposed. She was wearing white, tightly pulled panties. They were high on her hips and firmly pulled around the flesh of her cunt. She made a pointless attempt to close the open skirt and giggled at her failure.

'My name's Brooke. You can see what I like. I have to keep my skirt open like this — my cunt gets so hot.'

She lifted the open flap of her skirt and eased her fingers around the tightly covered slit of her cunt.

'Wow! So hot!'

The man whose cock bulged in his trousers stepped up and pressed his hand on top of hers. Her eyes widened as he massaged her cunt. He turned back and nodded to Maizie. She nodded back and the man led Brooke away.

The next two stepped forward together.

'We come together,' said the one in the shiny red evening dress.

'Yes! We come as a pair!' giggled the one in the tightly pleated short blue skirt.

'My name's Dahlia.'

'And mine's Lexy.'

Dahlia embraced Lexy. She opened her mouth and licked Lexy's cheeks. Lexy's smooth pale skin glistened with Dahlia's spit. Lexy opened her mouth and the two kissed each other forcefully and passionately. I felt a nervous thrill in my stomach as I watched them — their arms enfolding each other, their faces pressed together, their bodies writhing at the thrill of contact. I licked my dry lips.

One of the men had taken out his cock and was holding its stiff length in his hand. Lexy broke away from Dahlia and looked at him. Her lips dripped with spit. She dropped to her knees at the man's feet and slowly encircled the throbbing glans of his cock with her hungry mouth. Dahlia came up behind her and, bringing both her hands from behind and passing them beneath her armpits, placed them over Lexy's full breasts. She squeezed Lexy's nipples thought the soft material as Lexy dropped her head lower onto the man's cock. He lifted it into her mouth and she took it down into her throat until her lips were tightly around the base. She opened her eyes and stared up at him, blankly, her throat filled with his cock, writhing against Dahlia's ever tightening grip on her hard and prominent nipples. Her eyes widened, and her mouth was forced open as his cock expanded then, still staring into his face, she gulped as he filled her throat with his copious ejaculation.

She did not move back, she kept her wide eyes open. She gulped and swallowed and stayed sucking at his fluid until he dropped his hips back and sighed loudly with satisfaction. When finally she pulled away, she took an enormous gasping breath and held it in as she let the semen she had not swallowed dribble in a stream from her open glistening mouth.

Dahlia released her grip on Lexy's nipples. Lexy's mouth dropped wider and frothing semen flowed over her bottom lip. Dahlia reached her hands up, wiped them across Lexy's mouth then smeared the spit and semen across Lexy's eyes. Lexy kept her eyes open as the sticky semen ran around her eyelids, dripped from her eyebrows and oozed down onto her flushed cheeks.

The man stood up, wrapped his arms around both girls' waists and led them out.

'Come on,' said Maize. 'I'll show you more.'

I was startled. Suddenly, I realised I had my hand down the front of my jeans and my fingers in the crack of my cunt. I pulled my hand out quickly. My fingers were glistening with my moisture. My cheeks fleshed red.

Maizie nodded to the girl in the suit who was still standing at the door. The girl nodded back, as though acknowledging an unspoken instruction.

'Good!' said Maizie. 'Good!'

She led me down a red painted corridor to another door. The sign said, 'The Rodeo Bucking Bull'.

'I think you will find this interesting, my dear.'

She led me into a large room that was partitioned by a heavy red velvet curtain. The curtains were drawn. On the side we went into, raised up on a stage, was a moulded wooden and steel structure roughly in the shape of a bull. It had four legs with shiny steel hooves; the body was sculptured so that the narrow, rounded and dished-in back expanded at the heavy haunches and buttocks. Where the head would have been there was a smooth cupped section of wood with metal edges raised into two huge pointed horns. Braced between the bases of the two horns was an exposed shiny steel rod. Leather straps hung near the fetlocks of each leg, and two larger straps hung from fixtures at its belly. A bowl of water by its side had been used to wet the leather straps and droplets of water dripped from them onto the wooden floor. At the rear was a broad step, large enough for someone to stand on.

'Meet our famous Rodeo Bucking Bull,' said Maizie proudly.

She took my hand and led me up to it.

'Some of our gentlemen drive hundreds of miles for the pleasures of our bucking beast. Feel the sensuous curves of its loins, my dear, the smoothness of its back, and the sharpness of its horns.'

I ran my hands along the massive bull's back. It was so smooth. I had never felt anything like it before. My fingers ran across its surface without, in some sense, touching it at all. It was like the smoothest glass — there seemed no friction at all. My mouth went dry as I ran my hands down its legs and felt the soft and wet leather of the straps.

'See how it's mounted,' she said, pointing to a heavy steel hydraulic cylinder attached beneath the massive animal. 'It is through this that its movements are controlled. It bucks like no other bull. Here, Syra, lie upon it. See how it feels. Remove your clothes so that you can feel its smoothness.'

I pulled my T shirt up over my head. The girl with the black suit had suddenly re-appeared. She held out her hands and took it from me. I removed my jeans and panties and she took them from me as well. She stood back, holding my clothing across her outstretched forearms. She dropped her head slightly and looked at the floor. She was delicate and beautiful.

'Yes, go on,' urged Maizie.'

I could not resist it. I stood beside it — its smooth surface pressed against my waist. I ran my hands across its dished back and up its broad nape to the steel bar between its horns. I felt a shiver of excitement run through me as I realised my nakedness, and a further shiver as I felt again the smooth surface of the magnificent bucking bull.

The door, through which we had entered, opened. The four women I had seen earlier entered in a line. Lexy carried a small stool in her hands. She placed it by the side of the bucking bull and moved back. She stood on one side of the bull's head, Dahlia stood on the other, while Kristal and Brooke stood on either side of its hindquarters.

I looked across to Maizie. She nodded. I stood up on the step, ran my hands along the dished back of the beast, lifted my leg and straddled it. I leant forward and saw straight away why it was dished along its spine. I dropped myself down and found my hips, breasts and shoulders fitted it perfectly. My nipples pressed against the smooth surface and I licked my dry lips. I let my head down and straight away found my mouth against the steel rod that ran between the two massive horns. I reached up and grabbed them in my hands. I realised I needed more of what the beast could offer. And I knew that this would not be how I would be finally positioned. I pictured the wet leather straps on the beast's legs and knew that soon I would find myself secured within their tight grasp.

I opened my mouth and took the steel bar between my teeth — it was cold and smooth. I licked my tongue above and beneath it. My spit ran over its surface. I bit down and sucked against it. I felt my tingling nipples hardening even more against the hard shiny surface of the beast's shoulders. I breathed in heavily through my nostrils and imagined the snorting bull scraping the ground with his hooves.

I heard Maizie's voice, but I could not make out her words. I saw Lexy and Dahlia moving closer. They took my hands off the massive sharp horns. I kept the metal bar in my mouth as they lowered my hands down the sides of the front legs of the bull. They let them hang there for a few moments and I felt my shoulders slipping perfectly into the cupped shapes that were created for them in the animal's massive back.

I felt the leather straps being opened and wound around my wrists. The wet leather was soft and pliable and, when they pulled it up into the buckles, it felt slippery against my wrists.

I closed my eyes for a moment — imagining what I must look like, straddling the back of the huge bull, my mouth around the steel brace between its horns; my arms pulled down on each side and attached by wet leather straps to its heavy fetlocks.

I raised my buttocks and felt the naked flesh of my cunt sticking to the smooth surface of the beast's back. It tugged at my clitoris and I felt a sudden rush of excitement. I bit harder onto the steel bar and swallowed the foamy spit that now filled my mouth.

I felt hands holding my feet — they belonged to Kristal and Brooke. I saw a hint of Kristal's mauve swimsuit reflected on the shiny surface of one of the beast's horns as she bent forward, and a hint of Brooke's short white tennis skirt flashed quickly on the surface of the other. They drew my legs down on either side of the animal's hindquarters — pulling my thighs into the scooped out slots in the beast's side and splaying my buttocks wide. My cunt and anus were fully exposed — I felt so vulnerable. They pulled my feet down as far as they could and fixed them in the wet leather straps. They tugged the leather hard into the buckles and, I saw another flash of their clothing reflected in the horns as they stood back.

I was unwilling to let go of the bar in my mouth for a single moment and I panted heavily through my nostrils. The pressure of my forced breathing made me feel giddy. My heart was thumping, and I was shivering as waves of expectation and excitement ran through me. I stared ahead, now not daring, nor wanting, to close my eyes for a second. I waited, not knowing what it was that would follow, only knowing my situation meant I could not protect myself from anything that was decided about my fate by others. The thought of my exposure made me grip the bar between my teeth even tighter, and that made me pant even harder through my wide nostrils.

Suddenly, something was yanked around my waist. I tightened my teeth onto the steel bar and breathed in heavily through my flaring nostrils. It tightened more — it was the wet strap of leather that had been dangling beneath the belly of the beast. It was being pulled so tightly around my waist that I struggled to get my breath. I felt the end pulling through the buckle, tightening all the time, then, I felt it being pinned to the buckle pin to keep it in place. I was overwhelmed with anxiety as I realised, for the first time, the danger of my situation — naked, pinioned around the waist and fixed by my arms and legs to the heavy sculpted bucking bull. I struggled desperately for breath, fearful of what might happen next.

Again, I heard Maizie's voice. Reflected in the shiny

surface of the horns, I saw the heavy red curtains pulling back. An engulfing shiver of fear filled my stomach with uncontrollable nervousness.

Maizie shouted some instructions. Lexy and Dahlia moved back out of my sight. There was silence — I could hear only the pounding of my heart and the grinding of my teeth on the steel bar that was wedged firmly across my wide-stretched mouth. Then I felt a draught — a movement of air across the skin of my widespread buttocks. It cooled the skin in the open crack between them and caressed the flesh of my cunt and the muscular ring of my dilated anus. Then I felt something against my buttocks, something smooth. Then it was against my back, then my shoulders. It felt like leather — supple, smooth, and velvety. Then it brushed against the back of my neck and I saw Lexy and Dahlia again as they walked forward carrying in their hands a leather cloak and hood.

The four women spread the leather over me, draping its hood over my head, allowing it to fall down beside my own secured hands, and its bottom to hang down over my pinioned legs. I felt the weight of it and, when I breathed in, I smelled the tangy sharpness of freshly tanned leather. As the hood fell over me, everything went dark. I could no longer see any reflections in the horns. My nostrils filled with the tangy scent. I bit down harder on the steel bar.

I heard a muffled voice — I was not sure whose it was. I thought I heard footsteps behind me, but it was all too indistinct to make out. My hot breath engulfed my face, flushing my skin and causing sweat to break out across my forehead and cheeks. I opened my eyes and stared into the darkness beneath the leather — inhaling its bitter perfume, becoming part of it.

I felt the bottom of the cloak being lifted up, exposing my distended cunt. I imagined its glossy pinkness, the neat crack at its centre, the honeyed moisture running in the delectable central valley of its flesh. There was silence. I stared ahead. I bit harder onto the steel brace. My nostrils opened as wide as I could make them. My breath was heavy and panting. I snorted. I gulped at the copious flow of saliva that ran down my throat. I felt enveloped by an abyss of expectation and fear.

The first thing I felt was heat against the wide wet flesh of my cunt. It pressed against it. It was hard — it was the glans of a stiff throbbing cock. There was no resistance to its pressure — the touch itself let it in.

I breathed in heavily as it entered. It did not pause or pull back. It pushed into me until its head was against the highest point inside. It felt as though it touched my heart. It seemed to be pressing against it — throbbing, pulsating, and burning me with its heat. The shaft was venous and ribbed, and tugged at the inside of my flesh as its relentless pressure took it in. Then it stopped — at its deepest it stopped and throbbed inside me.

Its pulsating filled my whole body. I breathed in time with it, my heart beat with its pounding rhythm. It had filled me and taken me over.

I bit hard onto the steel brace in my mouth, but I could apply no more pressure. My mouth was full of saliva, and now it ran in streams from the corners of my widespread lips before streaming down either side of my chin. My whole body was heated beneath the cloak and hood and trickles of sweat ran down the sides of my thighs and my arms.

Then I felt an extra movement. It was beneath me — the bull was beginning to buck! At first it twisted to the side — which side I couldn't tell. Then it pitched forward, and then back. The movements became more violent, more sudden, more frantic. Still the hot cock in my cunt stayed in at its full length but now, with every gyration of the bucking bull, it pulled or tugged more brutally against the insides of my flesh, or pressed or forced itself even deeper than what had seemed its limits.

I gripped onto the steel bar with my teeth. I grasped the legs of the animal with my hands. I stared ahead into the hot scented darkness and, as the beast tossed and bucked wildly, I felt the flowing heat of semen as the cock inside me expanded into a thick fiery shaft that filled me completely.

Suddenly, I closed my eyes — it was all I could do as a massive throb of ecstasy ran inside me. It started at the end of the cock, where the hot semen flowed, but it spread out quickly, like a lava flow, until it touched every part of my convulsing body. I jerked against my bonds, I swallowed, I dribbled and then, unable to retain it any longer I released the bar.

I heard my cry and could not believe it was coming from me. It was the bellowing of an animal — the cry of a wild beast. I let it out and it filled my head. Saliva exploded from my mouth. The huge cock kept filling me with it massive flow and, at the same time as I continued to be plugged full by it, I was tossed and bucked in every direction, every angle by the frantic gyrations of the bucking bull. My orgasm met the pressures that each new angle presented — it was like a joining of forces. I howled again. I shouted for more. I screamed for less. I did not know what I was doing. I wallowed in my own unending pleasure as I bucked and reared in wild ecstatic circles of completely abandoned joy.

I was shaking when they lifted me down. I stared at the delectable fleshy valley caused by the tight pulled material of Kristal's swimsuit. As I looked at it I felt another jerking paroxysm of joy come over me. I wanted to reach my mouth forward and lick it, lick the material that covered her beautiful flesh, taste her cunt through the filmy mauve fabric, wet my lips with her succulent moisture.

As I lay on a red velvet sofa, still naked, still shaking, I watched the young woman in the suit, shirt and tie, paying money to Lexy, Dahlia, Kristal and Brooke. They each smiled as she pressed $100 notes into their hands. Maizie seemed especially pleased as a large wad of money was handed over.

'And this is for the new girl,' said the young woman. 'I was very pleased.'

I stayed at Maizie's for several weeks — I liked it there. I rode the bull three times a week — that was as much as I could stand — and in some ways more than I could stand. Each time was a new experience; each set of frantic movements a new and overwhelming exhilaration. My rides on the bucking bull took me to new levels of joy each time, and each time, after I had recovered, all I could think of was doing it again. The last time I rode it was the longest — I was strapped to it for several hours into the early hours of the morning. I don't know how many men came and took their position. I don't know how many times I shrieked with the pleasure of ecstasy their thrusting cocks brought on but, when they had all finished with me, I know I lay across the beast's back for hours. I was soaked with semen and it ran from my anus and cunt as I shivered and jerked, gripped with repeated orgasms of continuous joy. And I cried with pain. As they rode me they had thrashed me hard across my flanks with a riding crop, and had beaten me across my buttocks with a flailing leather strap. I couldn't even stand when finally they lifted me down. I lay in a jacuzzi for hours, staring into the warm mist rising from its surface, listening to the bubbles of water bursting around me — speaking to me of the pleasures of suffering and pain. I was hypnotised by them, lost in the painful elation of bliss that riding the bucking beast had brought to me. I imagined myself floating — caught in the vortex of a warm ecstatic waterfall. I realised that if I did not go now then I would never leave.

The next day I filled the pick-up with gas, drove off down the dusty road, and never looked back.

7. Luna Mesa
THE RACE

I drove along a lonely, high desert road. It was little more than a sliver of tarmac laid on rock. It ran for miles on a dizzying ridge parallel to Capitol Reef, the bleak, brush-covered scrubland where Butch Cassidy and the Sundance Kid, after carrying out brutal robberies in neighbouring Nevada, rode for cover in Hole in the Wall.

It was cold and dry. I had not seen another car for over fifty miles then, as if conjured up from the mythical Wild West itself, a roughly built, slab-sided timber structure appeared on my left. It had several scrap cars alongside —compulsory for every habitation in the area— a wide, empty porch and, emerging from its heavy stone chimney, a slowly rising wispy curl of wood smoke. A spacious parking area at the rear gave way to another building, like an assembly hall but completely windowless. An uncertain neon light hanging on rusty chains from the porch announced erratically 'Luna Mesa Open'.

I drew up and went inside. The air was cold and I went straight to the large black stove and lifted my hands to its warm iron surface. The room was filled with artefacts — some pinned to the walls or the beams, some in dusty glass cases, some collected in old crates and boxes. There were tickets, photographs, leather holsters, loose ammunition, boots, gloves, hats, paintings and drawings, and, in every other space, bunches of colourless dried flowers. Near the small serving hatch, a life-size effigy of John Wayne was surrounded by photographs of him posing with another man in front of the café in earlier, apparently more prosperous, days.

'That's my daddy there,' said a wild haired and heavily

dressed woman who came in from the kitchen accompanied by a blast of freezing air. 'There he is with the Duke himself. My name's Leanne. Are you looking for a good time? You must stay over for the dance.'

I felt confused. She pointed to a bright notice by the door — 'Barn Dance Tonight'.

'What do you think?' she asked eagerly. 'It's good fun. Lots of spunky men. Lots of music. Lots of anything you fancy. All good clean cowboy fun.'

'Yes.' I said. 'Why not?'

'Good choice. I'll get you something to eat. You look half-starved. Some toast and grits will set you up.'

I sat by the stove and ate my meal — 'grits' with everything. I finished quickly — I was hungry and the food was good — put my empty plate on the floor, and went to sleep.

The next thing I knew it was dark and there was loud music exploding in my ears. I wiped my eyes, and still felt bleary with sleep as I walked over to the large windowless barn. The car park behind it was filled with pick-ups. Men in jeans and T shirts drank beer from cans and congregated in small jostling groups. A couple of young women — I could only see their long hair and cowboy hats — ran between ranks of men. They were involved in some sort of race. The men cheered and threw their hats in the air as the women raced for a finishing line held out by two of the men. I climbed up on the back of a pick-up to see more closely. I opened my eyes wide as I saw that the women were wearing only their panties, and the men ranked on each side of the 'race course' were whipping them with riding crops and leather belts.

I leant forward on the cab top of the pick-up. Another race was starting. Two fresh women were pushed forward.

They too were both naked except for their panties — pulled high onto their hips and drawn tight against the flesh of their cunts. Men pushed each other to get to the front of two lines on each side of the track. It was lit up by lights from pick-ups and extended the full width of the car park to a strung out finishing line of red and white plastic barrier tape.

The women looked frightened — cowering and ducking their heads — as the men nearest to them prodded and taunted them. Some men spat at them and the women's faces glistened with running saliva. Several men stood behind them with riding crops and leather straps. One of the men flicked a thin strap across one the women's buttocks. She flinched and tried to turn away. The men around her pushed her back and she was strapped again. She had nowhere to go except forward. She looked terrified.

Suddenly a gun was fired — I saw the smoke from it amongst the crowd of men. A cheer went up and the women were driven forward. Men on each side of the track smacked their buttocks and the men behind flayed them with the straps and crops.

The terrified women ran as fast as they could towards the finishing tape. One of them stumbled. Her legs fell wide apart as she hit the ground. I could see the dark valley cut by her panties as they were pulled tightly into the deep crack of her fleshy cunt by the fall. She scrambled to get up but, by the time she was on her feet, the other woman had run headlong through the tape.

The winner was lifted high on the men's shoulders and paraded amongst the excited crowd. The loser was dragged from the track by her ankles. They pulled her panties down to her knees. She struggled against them, but there were too many of them. They yanked her panties down over her ankles and splayed her legs wide. Her cunt was fleshy and wet. She twisted her hips from side to side, but they just laughed at her desperate and pointless efforts.

They flipped her over onto her front. Her buttocks were rounded and muscular. A leather strap was brought down on them. She flinched and tried to wriggle away, but again her efforts only brought more laughter and derision. One of the men knelt between her legs and forced her buttocks wide. I saw the dark centre of her anus and, beneath it, the glistening sparkle of her wet cunt. He wrapped his arm beneath her hips and lifted her buttocks high. The others cheered as he brought his hand down flatly on her smooth upturned and exposed skin. The contact made a loud slap and almost immediately I saw a red smudge appear where the smacking hand had landed. Another slap, another red smudge, and the woman yelled out so loudly that I could hear her scream clearly above the roaring taunts and jeers of the men.

Another man jumped down beside the first. He pushed him off and took his position. He was wearing jeans with light brown leather chaps hanging down from a leather belt at his waist. He unzipped his trousers and took out his hard throbbing cock. He held the end of it against the woman's now-dilated anus. He pulled his hand along the venous shaft. The woman squirmed but, as soon as she moved, he pushed his cock into her anus. She reared up in terror and he pushed it in more. She lifted her buttocks higher and, in one long thrust, his cock went in up to the base.

As many as wanted took turns, some thrashing her buttocks with straps and belts, some smacking her with their hands, some bringing down cutting slashes with a riding crop. One took his leather chaps off and flayed them across her squirming back. Most of them drove their cocks into her anus and some of them used her cunt as well. They drenched her with their semen, splashing it over her back, between her shoulder blades and in her hair. They turned her over and filled her mouth with it and then, even as she continued to writhe and twist against their powerful gripping hands, I saw that she swallowed it in long luxuriating gulps.

For a moment, she was released, no one was holding her down and straight away she got up onto her knees and took the cock nearest to her face into her open semen-filled mouth. She sucked at it and ran her hands along its length then, as she opened her eyes wide and semen frothed in her nostrils, she swallowed the cock down as deeply into her throat as it would go.

She coughed and choked as it came out. She sat on her knees with semen running from her mouth, dripping from her chin and covering her breasts. It trickled from the ends of her hard nipples as she scrambled forward on her knees anxious to reach out to get another cock into her hands and then into her hungry, gaping mouth.

They forced her to her feet and, whipping her with leather belts, they made her run the rest of the way to the finishing line which was now crumpled on the dusty ground. Semen ran down the insides of her thighs as she ran as fast as she could beneath the rain of their punishing blows.

I bit onto my lips and swallowed hard — my mouth was dry. I reached down between the tops of my thighs and curled my fingers up against the denim that covered my cunt. I felt its heat through the material and started undoing the belt so that I could get my fingers against its naked flesh.

Suddenly, I realised I had been seen.

'There's someone else who wants to play!'

'It sure looks like it! Look! She's started without us!'

I ducked down behind the cab and crouched on the corrugated floor of the pick-up deck. I was panting hard and my heart was beating wildly. I realised I still had my fingers in my cunt. Their pressure was sending thrills of delight right up into my chest. Crouching down had wedged them inside and they were pressed hard against the swollen flesh. I drew them back and felt the warm wetness of moisture that ran down them. As several men clambered up onto the back of the pick-up, I ducked my head in a ridiculous effort to hide.

'Well you're a pretty sight. Welcome to the dance. May I have the pleasure?'

He held out his hand. I felt deeply embarrassed. I squirmed and removed my fingers from my cunt. Hurriedly, I buckled up my belt, and leant back against the rear of the cab. Three men stood in front of me. One of them stepped forward and held out his hand. He was dressed in jeans, a red and white checked shirt and cowboy boots. Light brown leather chaps hung from his belt by thin leather thongs. He urged his hand forward and I took it. He helped me down from the back of the pick-up and threw his arm around my waist.

'Turkey in the Straw!' he shouted.

An accordion and fiddle broke into a hectic and urgent tune. Heads bobbed and bounced, and skirts swung in wide circles as the hoedown began.

My partner stamped and high-stepped, twisted and turned. He flung me around him, holding me by my waist or lifting my hands up high and spinning me in a tight circle. I felt dizzy and confused. Everything was spinning. The fiddle got louder, its double-stopped, Cajun-like screech making it impossible to think clearly. As if compelled by the magic of the music my partner danced me out through the door and into the centre of the crowded, noise filled car park. The musicians followed and the other revellers ran behind.

Suddenly, a long narrow gap appeared in the midst of the dancing — two lines of men quickly formed on each side of it. The manic fiddling continued, but the dancing abated. My partner flung me in a circle for the last time, held me by the waist, bent me backward, leant over and kissed me hard on the mouth. He released me and spun me away from him. I fell backwards into the hands of the men that lined one side of the empty space that lay between them and the other line.

They pulled my T shirt up over my head. I felt a sudden chill against my exposed nipples — they hardened and tingled. I was flung sideways and lifted from the ground. My belt was unbuckled and pulled free of my jeans. The button at the top of the zip was undone then the zip was pulled down. For a moment, I was not sure whether I had panties on or not. I saw them fleetingly as my jeans were ripped down and pulled away — I felt a strange sense of misplaced safety. My head fell backwards but I felt the thin material tugging at the flesh of my cunt as my panties were roughly removed and thrown down on the dirty ground. They lifted me, naked, above their heads and paraded me like a trophy to the incessant hypnotic high-pitched drone of the frenzied fiddle.

They pulled my legs wide. I felt the cold air against the warm flesh of my cunt. I felt the exposure of my slit to their gaze — to their presence, their mockery and taunts. Hands clawed at my breasts, fingers pinched my nipples. I felt a finger probing into my anus, and one running along the fleshy crack of my naked cunt. A wave of fear came over me. My head was spinning.

A flash of light made me squeeze my eyelids tightly together. The headlights of pick-ups parked around the car park already provided illumination, but now, headlights mounted on their cabs had been turned on, and I found myself bathed in a dazzling blaze of white light.

I was dragged over to the end of the lines of men. They jeered at me as I was pulled along, struggling against their grip, twisting pointlessly in an effort to release myself. Another woman stood there waiting. She was naked too. Her long blonde hair fell in tangles onto her square shoulders. Her tear-filled eyes were blackened with moist eye shadow. Her hard nipples stood out prominently from her full breasts — both reddened where she had been mishandled, slapped and pinched. She looked over to me anxiously but, as soon as our eyes met, she was roughly turned around to face away from me.

We were made to stand side by side facing in the opposite direction to the lines of men. I felt the heat of her body. When I tried to glance across at her, the men grabbed my head and made me face forward. They pulled my hands down by my sides. Men in leather jeans and wearing leather chaps pushed against me. The leather slid smoothly against my skin and its scent filled my nostrils. As I stared ahead, I realised that it had gone quiet — the fiddling had stopped, the dancing was over.

I felt something against my shoulders — something

pliable, something leather. They pulled a strap over each shoulder and, as they tightened them both into buckles between my naked breasts, I felt something tighten across the back of my shoulders. I glanced sideways at the other woman. They were doing the same to her. They were fitting harnesses to us!

They pulled the straps so tight I could hardly breathe. The leather harness straps pulled across my breasts, a split in the straps was pulled over my nipples so that they were pinched in between the split leather. My nipples ached with the pain but they hardened and throbbed as the straps were pulled up hard into the buckles and the leather was tightened even more around them. I heard the other woman gasp as they brought the straps up to their limit in the buckles. I saw a dribble of sparkling spit run from the corner of her mouth and the glistening glitter of her tear-soaked cheeks.

A metal bit was pulled across my mouth. It clanked against my teeth and I gasped as they pulled it tightly. It squeezed my mouth wide and pressed back into my distorted cheeks. I gasped for breath, and my nostrils flared as I fought desperately to suck in air. They tied the bit with three leather straps — one passing over the top of my head, the other two pulled around my head, pinching my ears. They twisted the three straps together at the back of my neck making them so tight I couldn't move my tongue. I wanted to shriek, to cry out, but my gasping panic and fearful wide eyes were the silent testament to my unreleased terror.

Spit ran over my chin as I was turned around to face down between the lines of men. They leant forward and jeered. I was shivering with fear. The woman next to me was crying. One of the men smacked her on the buttocks with a leather belt and remonstrated with her, but it only made her worse. Saliva dribbled profusely from her mouth and she was shivering all over. I saw for the first time how beautiful she was — tall and angular, with high cheekbones and dark wide eyes. Even terrified as I was, I felt a tingling surge of excitement seeing her with the harness strapped to her naked shoulders, the metal bit pulled tightly across her mouth, her tear-filled eyes, and her lean smooth-skinned limbs. Her pubic hair had been shaved and the top of her cunt was visible as a delectable notch in the smooth flesh that led down to it. A sudden smack on my buttocks made me turn around and face forward down the line of men.

I looked into the dazzling lights. Shadows of men sitting on the cab tops of pick-ups looked like terrible phantoms in a burning hell of terror. Then it went black. Suddenly, I could see nothing. A heavy bag had been pulled over my head. I gasped for breath. I felt the heat of moist air around my face. I was filled with panic. I opened my eyes wide and stared into the consuming darkness. My heart was pounding loudly in my chest. I tried to swallow, but it was impossible — my spit just ran down my chin in streams.

I felt a weight against my shoulders and something straining against me, or me straining against it — I wasn't sure. I leant forward slightly and felt the resistance of something behind me. I did not understand what it was. My confusion made me giddy. I felt faint. I thought I would pass out. The jeering of the men turned into a muffled drumming as I struggled for breath and fought to keep myself conscious.

A flash of light made me reel as the bag was pulled from my head. I couldn't see anything. A biting pain on my buttocks made me reel. Another, this time sharper and even more painful, made me lurch forward. Another, and I wanted to scream. I took a pace forward and felt the weight behind me. Another cutting stroke and my skin burnt. Another and another. I took a full pace forward. I looked to the side. I still couldn't see properly, but now I could just make out the shape of the other woman and behind her a small pony trap, attached to the harness at her shoulders.

We were in a race, and we had no choice but to run — the men behind us were flailing at us with crops and belts. They struck our buttocks and backs with stinging cuts. Some of the flailing leather licked around our necks or caught our shoulders or the backs of our arms. I ran as fast as I could. At first, I could hardly move the weight of the trap but, as it got going, it was easier. The men ran after us, lashing us, beating us, and we both ran on matching each other's pace, trying to escape our punishers, forced to compete for victory.

The men lining either side of the course leant out and cheered us on. Some of them spat on us, some of them urinated on us. I felt the sting of their urine on my legs as it mixed with the heat of my skin, my own sweat and the coldness of the night air.

We raced on even faster. I bit onto the metal in my mouth. I slurped at the spit that ran from each side. I opened my nostrils as wide as they would go and drew in huge long breaths. I saw the red and white finishing line. I felt the pain of my tormentor's lashing straps. I raced on. I saw the other woman falling back. I sensed I would win. I bit harder on the steel rod in my mouth and lurched forward in a sudden burst of strength. The weight on my shoulders seemed to be pushing me. The pain of the clasping split strap around my nipples seemed to be drawing me forward. I felt as though the bit in my mouth was pulling me towards the only thing I could see — the finishing line, and my ultimate victory.

I burst through the tape and fell forward against my harness. I had won!

Hands pawed at me. I felt fingers in my cunt, and in my anus. I wanted them inside me. I wanted to be defiled. I shook my head — neighing in victory. Spit flew from my mouth in a shower. I shook my head again. Just watching the saliva bursting into the cold air in a sparkling shower filled me with excitement. I flexed my arms wide. I wriggled against the cutting straps around my nipples. I opened my legs and welcomed the probing fingers. I let my wetness run onto them. I squeezed myself down onto them. I buried them inside me. I sat my anus on the others, taking them deep, wriggling on them, being exhilarated by their penetration — thinking of nothing else except how they filled me.

My harness was released and I dropped to the floor. I lay on my back. Cocks were in front of my face. I watched their semen splashing down on me. I moved myself so that it would come into my eyes. I blinked on it, letting it run beneath my eyelids, blurring my vision, satiating me with its sticky delight. Some of it ran along the bit in my mouth. I tasted its saltiness. I tried to drink it but it lay on my outstretched lips, unavailable, tantalising me with its scent and only the vaguest hint of its flavour.

Urine poured down on me. It washed my eyes, stinging them as it cleared them of the sloppy mass of semen that had run over them and blinded me. It ran up my nostrils, into my ears and over my breasts. I rolled in it, soaking myself in its golden rain, bathing in it, drowning in it, as

I drove myself repeatedly onto the fingers that filled me and which brought me suddenly to a massive exploding orgasm. My eyes were filled with a sparkling storm. My body and my mind were overtaken by it. I did not know where I was, what I was doing. I wanted violating more. I wanted humiliating more. I wanted only to be the subject of the wishes of others. I fell on my side and, in a blaze of dazzling light and the throes of overpowering jerks of passion, I descended into a maelstrom of confusion, degradation, and delight.

Leanne came out as I sat on the porch. She grinned broadly and gathered the wide neck of her thick jumper around her neck. She was clutching a pile of still-wet photographs.

'You had a good time last night, sweetie? I can see that!'

She went to the bright notice that advertised the barn dance. She started pinning the photographs around it. She turned some of them at different angles and peered at them diligently.

'I sure as hell can see that!'

She dropped one of the photographs and hurriedly bent to pick it up. It was a picture of me! I flushed red with embarrassment.

Leanne laughed and carried on with her task.

A car drove up. A pretty young woman got out and walked up to the porch. She was underdressed for the cold and shivered as she pushed the door open.

Leanne pointed inside at the photographs which surrounded the life-sized image of John Wayne.

'That's my daddy there,' she said proudly. 'There he is with the Duke himself. My name's Leanne. Are you looking for a good time? You must stay over for the dance. All good clean cowboy fun.'

I ran to the pick-up. I was filled with a deep sense of humiliation. I had been made a fool of. As I opened the door of the pick-up and climbed in, my mind was filled with the degrading pictures of me, stuck clumsily to the poster on the wall of the porch.

'Byee!' someone shouted behind me.

I turned. It was the beautiful woman I had raced against. She was standing with Leanne. They had their arms draped around each other's shoulders.

'See you again sometime!' she shouted. 'If you're ever passing this way.'

8. LAS VEGAS
THE HIGHEST BID

I drove for hours but still the humiliating pictures of me on the barn wall stayed burnt into my mind. They had played a cruel trick on me, and I had been so innocent, so willing to fall into their trap.

I saw the images of myself, rolling on the dirty ground, covered in semen and urine, half conscious, craving, and screaming for more. That I could not remember exactly what had happened made it worse. Each image had filled me with a sense of undirected guilt. And I had seen them all — in one horrifying burst they had imprinted themselves on my mind. I had been unable to avoid them — I had soaked them all up in one go. I could not avoid them or pretend. I knew it was me, but I did not know how it had happened, how I had let it happen. But of course I had not 'let it happen'. I had lost control. My passion and need had taken me over. And it had hurled me into a world beyond satisfaction, a world where nothing was enough — a world where I most wanted to be. I knew that, but the sting of humiliation and shame was all the worse for it. Pictures of the men parading me — dirt covered, head hung in shame — made me shiver. Images of me being dragged behind a pick-up, my face tortured with an insatiable need for more caused my mouth to go dry. Seeing myself rolling in their urine — rubbing it on my face and body, and all the time crying out for more — just made me just want to run and hide.

I was suddenly overcome with a wave of desire. I stopped the car and drove my fingers into my cunt. I probed them deeply and rapidly as, in a frenzied burst of uncontrolled and violent passion, I fought desperately to exorcise the images from my mind. I lay across the plastic covered bench seat gasping noisily — my fingers sloppy with wetness from my cunt, my wet lips overflowing with a stream of frothy spit, my head filled with images of my own degradation. I felt completely debauched as I splayed myself wide. I slapped the palm of my hand repeatedly against the exposed wet flesh of my cunt. It was a way of punishing myself, reprimanding myself, but it did not work. The sound of my smacking hand against my wet cunt only inflamed me more and, as I smacked the smarting flesh harder, I rose up against it, craving more, opening myself for more. My frantic cries echoed inside the car as glistening tears of joy ran in streams down my reddened cheeks.

The sun got higher and it got hotter as I drove through the flat-roofed town of Mesquite. I pulled off at Glendale and parked on a rocky desert ridge overlooking Lake Mead. I stared at the twisting lake as it snaked its way through the orange desert south towards the Hoover Dam.

I still felt the wetness of my cunt, and the stinging from my violated flesh. I squeezed my legs together in a pointless effort to mask my need, as an uncontrollable surge of excitement ran between my hips. I knew that still I was not satisfied. I opened my mouth and spit ran onto my chin. I sucked it back, rolled it over my tongue then blew it out between my lips in noisy frothing bubbles. I just wanted to be violated — that was all I could think of.

I threw myself across the bench seat and tore down the zip of my jeans. I yanked them down to my knees — just enough to expose my white panties. My heart was thumping loudly. I was panting in noisy erratic bursts. I stared down at the white material that covered my cunt.

I licked my tongue out towards the smooth mound and the indentation at its centre which heralded the crack of my flesh. I strained to reach it, pushing out my tongue as far as it would go. Suddenly, unable to hold back any longer, I pulled my panties down and ran my fingers across the smooth skin around the naked glistening slit. The warm plastic of the seat pressed stickily against my taut buttocks. The images of how I had been shown up at Luna Mesa — how I had been ridiculed and humiliated — flashed through my mind. My face flushed as I thought of it, but my probing fingers found the sweet moist valley of my cunt and I rose up on them as the very shame I felt drove me once more to satisfy the passion it aroused in me.

Towards evening, I drove back up onto the I15 and turned left in the direction of the tempting sign — 'Las Vegas 33 Miles'.

The lights of Las Vegas were blinding — bright, flashing, endless. I drove down Las Vegas Boulevard. It was crowded with anxious bustling people eager to spend their money and find entertainment. I turned right between the glazed skyscrapers of New York New York and the fairytale towers of Excalibur and, distracted by the dazzling brilliance of it all, I rammed my pick-up into the side of a lumbering tourist bus.

I was thrown forward and banged my head against the steering wheel. Everything became confused. I heard voices and sensed hectic activity around me, but I really didn't know what was going on. The next thing I knew I was lying down on a large sofa in a red-curtained room with several women fussing over me.

'You've had a nasty shock, sweetie. You've got a real bump.'

One of the women bent down and looked closely into my eyes. She was young and beautiful. She wore a short bottle-green and black skirt, a neatly pressed white shirt and a green tie that matched the satiny sheen of her skirt. Her well formed legs ran down to shiny black leather shoes with pencil-width high heels. She smiled broadly, exposing her fine white teeth between her full and succulent lips.

'I think you should lie down for a while. My name's Crystal. I'll keep you company. It's good to sit down when you've had a shock. Would you like to hear how I found my way here?'

Her childish directness was captivating.

'Yes, I would,' I said, realising as soon as I moved that my neck ached and I felt a dizzy.

'Great! Let me get comfortable. Now, where shall I begin? Of course, the night he picked me up. Well, to be more exact, the night he won me!'

She pushed herself close to me. Her thighs were athletic and tanned. She folded up her legs enough to bring her feet off the floor. She pushed her shoes off one at a time with her toes. I smelled her sweetness.

'That's better! These heels are so high! But I have to wear them. No choice.'

She rubbed her calves and smiled again. She had beautiful teeth and the tip of her pink tongue poked out over them tantalisingly.

'Now, where was I? Nowhere! Of course! Right, the night he won me. Wow! It seems an age ago! Are we sitting comfortably? Good, then I'll begin.'

She laughed and pushed herself closer. I felt the warmth of her body. She looked down and brushed the front of her white shirt with the back of her hand.

'I hate wearing a bra. Don't you?'

I nodded absently.

'Was I in an accident?' I asked.

'Just a bump, sweetie. No damage. Right, this was what happened. I'm from Tennessee — what a drag! I couldn't get out quick enough. My daddy liked my sister and me a bit too much. You know what I mean. One day, when he was at church, I stole my brother's wallet and hitched a ride to Vegas. I walked into the first casino I came to — New York New York. In case you hadn't realised, that's where we are now. I couldn't believe the size of the place, and the glitz, and the girls, and so many people spending so much money. You'd think it grew on trees. I sat at a fruit machine — with the other schmucks. Ten minutes later I'd lost all the money I had. What a swindle! An old woman next to me was scooping it up into a bucket. I don't mind telling you, for a moment I thought of robbing the old bitch. She's still there now — she's on the payroll, of course. There are ten of them in this casino alone — just to encourage the punters.

'Anyway, I hadn't sat there for long and this guy comes up to me. He was sort of swarthy looking. He'd got a black patch over his one eye. Can you believe it! He looked like some sort of a pirate! He asks me if I'd like to earn some money. If I'd like to make up my losses. "Sure Thing," I said. "Sure thing." I'd need to do what I was told, he said, but if I could, well, if I could... He cocked his head to the side and looked at me knowingly. I hadn't got a clue what he meant, but I went with him anyway. When you're desperate it doesn't much matter. We walked across the main floor of the casino. I hadn't realised it was so big. I mean, I thought it was big when I came in, but I'd only got a part way into it. He walked ahead and I followed. I felt like some sort of slave, following him like that. He never looked back, he just expected me to do what he had said. He led the way into a room behind a heavy leather-padded door.

'Five men sat at a table. I can tell you, they looked like something out of the Godfather. They all held their cards tightly in their hands. One stared at the others, another looked at the money on the table, two of them stared at their cards, and the last had his eyes completely closed.

'"Sit down," the one with his eyes closed said. How did he know I was there? That's what I wanted to know. If he had his eyes closed, how did he know I was there? The man who'd brought me in nodded to him. Anyway, I sat and they played. Every so often they reached forward and pushed some money into the middle of the table. I can tell you, I don't know what they were doing. It was all beyond me. Suddenly the one who had his eyes closed when I came in, Jake they called him, smacked his fist down on the table. The piles of money scattered everywhere. It was a bit fractious, that's for sure.

'"Alright then," he said. "If my money's not good enough, what is?"

'The others looked at me.

'"Jake, if you've got no more money. What about the girl?"

'He looked me up and down. I felt his stare go right through my clothes. I realised I had no panties on. My face went red.

'"Okay," he said. "If the girl sucks your cock, is that enough?"

'"If she swallows it down as well, yes."

'Then he tells me outright, not "ask", you understand, but just tells me.

"'Suck his cock,' he says, just like that. And make sure when he comes that you swallow it all. We don't want to see any left over. A bet's a bet. Now get on with it. Go on! Get on with it!"

'For a moment, I hesitated. I thought, who the hell's this guy telling me what to do like that? But, well, you know, I hadn't got a dime. What else could I do?

'Well, I got down on my knees and took this guy's cock out. It was really big — stiff as a rod and a really venous shaft — and the end, that was swollen and really purple and throbbing. As I put it between my lips I thought it would burn me — it was so hot. I ran my tongue around that hard end. It tasted really good. I sucked it hard. I closed my eyes. I was enjoying it — no doubt about that. Suddenly, he grabbed my hair. He told me to open my eyes and look up at him, and so I did. He told me to hold my lips at the back of the glans and then rub my hands along the shaft "Five times!" he said. "No more! No less!" Well, I did what I was told, exactly what I was told.

'When he finished I sucked it all down. I didn't think of doing anything else. I just felt totally obedient. There was a lot of it, his semen, and it was like drinking, and I really enjoyed it — the whole lot. It was because of the way I had been taken there, I think. The way I had been told to do it, and the way I had just done it — never asked any questions, just done it. Being under control like that had thrilled me so much. I'd never done anything like it before. Well I wouldn't would I? Coming from Tennessee an' all. Anyway, I kept his cock in my mouth, even after I had swallowed all his semen. Yes, I kept it there, just looking up at him, waiting for him to tell me I could pull away. He made me wait for quite a while. And I waited. Then he reached down and opened my mouth.

He pulled his still hard cock out between my lips. He looked inside my mouth until he was satisfied there was no semen in it. Then he closed it, pinched my left cheek between his thumb and forefinger, dropped back onto his seat and carried on with the game. They all ignored me. I just stayed there on my knees — waiting to see if I was needed for anything else. When I swallowed, I could still taste the metallic saltiness of his semen. What a mouthful! What a beautiful mouthful!

'That's how it all started. So what happened next? Well, Jake was some sort of boss. He told the man with the patch to find me a room in the hotel. I thought that was the end of it — my reward for helping him out — but, sister, how wrong can you be!'

'It was a great room. I'd never been in one like that before. It was more a suite — it had its own sitting room. And what a bath! I made the best of it, I can tell you. Then, in the middle of the night I was woken by some goon who was standing over the bed. I tell you what, my heart was really thumping when I saw him there, leering down at me. I nearly died when I saw his patch! Anyway, he made me dress and took me down to the gaming room again. They were still there, and the piles of money — coins, notes and coloured chips— were even higher. Jake had his eyes closed again, his lids were heavy and dark.

'"Glad you could join us again," he said, not opening his eyes or turning around. I swear he had telepathy or second sight! "You've already been placed," he said, "as a bet." I obviously looked confused. Or maybe I gave him the impression that I thought I had done everything he wanted, and my night in the hotel room was my reward. Anyway, he left me in no doubt. I was his. He had bought me — and I'd better do everything he wanted.

'"Just do as you're told," he said.

'I stripped off and climbed up onto the table as he ordered. He told me to get down on my hands and knees with my bottom towards him. I did as he said. I knew he was looking at my cunt and anus. I opened my legs a bit so that he got a good view. It excited me to know what he was doing. I felt my anus dilating. It was so exciting. Really, I just couldn't help it.

'I waited on the table, just like that — naked with my bottom exposed. I didn't know whether to look at the men, or look down. He had not said anything about that. I looked down. I felt myself trembling, but I did not dare move again. I knew I must wait for an instruction. I don't know how, but I just knew it. Then it came, not an instruction, but a sudden, painful smack across my upturned bottom.

'I gasped as I was knocked forward. I still knew I should not move and I made sure I stayed where I was. It was a weird sensation, soaking up the power of the smack, absorbing it somehow. And I can tell you it was mighty hard! I kept my eyes down. I thought it was the right thing to do. Another smack, and wow, it hurt! It was sharp and quick, but it landed hard and it stung. My, did it sting! Still, I didn't allow myself to get knocked from the position he had told me to take on my hands and knees. I'd been spanked before, but never like this. This time I knew I could only react if I was told. There was no way I was going to cry out, or scream. No fear. I don't know why I knew — I just knew.

'Then one of them wound a blindfold across my eyes. Still I didn't move. I kept my eyes open beneath it, but it was a piece of heavy black cloth and I couldn't see any light at all.

'I listened to them counting the smacks — it was part of the bet, so many smacks for such-and-such a wager. Jake was betting me in the game and this time it was my naked bottom that was the stake.

'I ground my teeth together — I heard them grinding — it was my way of keeping my screams back. And I kept my mouth tight closed. I panted through my wide nostrils. But still I stayed where I had been told. Still I suffered my punishment with no sound, still I allowed myself to be humiliated because I was under the instruction of Jake.

'There was a pause. I heard raised voices — some argument over the deck. I heard a new pack being called for and the cellophane being torn from it. Then I felt the cellophane being stuffed in my mouth and I heard the jeers of the men as they mocked my predicament, and then the spanking started again.

'I think it might have been light by the time they finished. I heard them leave the room — slapping each other on the shoulders, congratulating themselves on their winnings or bemoaning their losses. I waited on the table. I didn't know what else to do. I felt frozen to the spot. It was weird. I knew there was no one there but still I waited for someone to instruct me to get down. I thought of running my hand along my crack — it was so hot and wet — but I didn't dare. I just waited.

'My arms ached, and I felt my legs tightening with cramp, but still I waited. My back and neck ached but I did not move. I started to see stars and flickering lights in front of my eyes. Every now and again my heart started beating fast and I breathed harder but, after a while, it passed. Spit ran around my mouth, but I kept the cellophane where it had been stuffed and only swallowed when my mouth was completely full of saliva. I felt the sensation of my bladder filling. Yes, I started to want a pee! But I knew straight away that would not make me move. I let it flow down the insides of my thighs. It gathered on the table and, before it soaked into the green baize surface, it formed pools around my knees. I smelled it for ages in my nostrils but, as time went on, it passed.

'I don't really remember anything else until I heard the door open. The same voices I had heard leaving came back into the room. They laughed at what they saw and I knew my face reddened as I realised my degrading position. But still I did not move — it had become my earnest duty to remain where I had been placed. Staying where I had been told was all that I had in my mind. It was my unalterable commitment. I had lost any will to do otherwise.

'I listened for a new order but it didn't come. There was more smacking, more pain and stinging on my buttocks, but no more instructions, no reason to move, nothing to tell me to change what was happening. And, you know, never for a single moment did I think I couldn't stand it. Never for one second did I think I couldn't go on, that I was wishing for it all to stop. No, can you believe it? It was incredible!

'The game ended. My bottom was so sore. I knew it was red, purple, bruised by the smacking hands of the eager gamblers. I heard the chairs being pushed back.

'"Get down," he said. "Take the blindfold off. And take that stuff out of your mouth. It's disgusting! You can sleep in the corner."

'I curled up in the corner of the room. It was cold. There was nothing to cover myself with, and, anyway, he had not told me I could do that even if there was. I pressed my naked bottom against the wall — it was quite cool and it took some of the sting away from my burning skin.

'I lay there naked and shivering. I ran my hands between my thighs, at first to keep them warm but, as soon as I realised how close they were to my cunt, I found a different reason for them to be there. I stayed curled up as he had told me, but I lifted my one leg slightly, just enough to get my hand up against my cunt. I pulled my fingers along the crack — it opened at my slightest touch. The soft flesh was wet and my finger ran along it easily. The crack just opened. I thrilled at the soft touch — it sent shivering tremors right up through my body. I pushed my fingers in and stayed like that — not moving, just enjoying them being inside me for the rest of the night.

'There was another session — just the same — then he told me to follow the man with the patch over his eye back to the bedroom. I slept for ages. I got up and bathed then went back to sleep. I think he must have known I was tired.

'After a while I began to wonder when I would be summoned again. I started to feel disappointed that I had been left alone, that he might not have any more use for me. When the man with the patch on his eye came for me I felt really relieved. I followed him back to the room behind the leather-padded door. This time it was different.

'The game was already underway, but there was no good humour between the players. They shouted at each other and angrily banged their hands down on the green baize table. This time, after the man with the patch stripped me naked, they made me lie on my back on the table. For a while I had to hold a pack of cards in my mouth. After that, one of them sloshed a glass of rye on the rocks over my face. Jake had told me not to move, so I just stayed there and took it. The heavy spirit ran down my cheeks and I could smell it as it dripped from my ears and down my neck. An ice cube lay in the indentation at my throat. It was freezing!

'When Jake increased his bet, the others took turns at pushing their fingers into my cunt. Later they all probed my anus. Jake got angry with them when they refused to accept his next proposal and he jeered at them until they finally acceded.

'They took me from the table, tied my ankles together and pulled me up on a rope attached to the central chandelier. My head hung just above the baize surface. I spun for ages until one of them stopped me. He drew my face towards his cock and stuck it deep into my mouth. I choked but he pushed it in deeper. Each took their turn; driving their cocks in as far as they could into my throat.

'As the bets got higher, the players became more insistent and demanding. One of them finished in my throat. Again, to start with, I choked but, once I started to swallow his semen, the choking stopped. They put cards into my mouth and, spinning me on the rope, passed them around between each other.

'I felt dizzy and sick, but they gave me no rest. One of them stood on his chair and urinated in my mouth. I spluttered as it streamed between my lips. I was not sure if I was to drink it, and Jake gave me no instructions. I swallowed all I could and let some of it run out up my nostrils and into my eyes. The others stood up on the table and urinated over my buttocks and cunt. It ran down my body and over my face until it dripped off my hair onto the table. My eyes stung with it and I reeked of its tangy scent.

'Finally, they released me and Jake told me to go and sleep in the room again. The next time I was brought down each of them bent me over the edge of the table and drove his cock into my cunt. This time, as the stakes got higher, they used my anus and, finally, I had two of their cocks in my mouth at the same time, one in my anus and one in my cunt. They came one at a time. The first finished in my cunt. I felt frantic as its heat filled me deep inside. Then the next came in my mouth and I sucked and swallowed ravenously. Then the other in my mouth hardened, swelled and suddenly sprayed its splashing semen over my tongue and into the back of my throat. My mouth was full of it. I slurped at it, eager to get every drop, desperate to quench my thirst for its delightful sticky milk. Then, in the end, and driving it as far as possible into my anus, I felt the sudden explosive hotness of the last one's copious semen as it burst deeply into my rectum. I squeezed myself tightly onto it, sucking at it, drawing and squeezing his cock until it was completely dry.

'I dropped back — gasping, dripping with sweat and semen, unable to recover. Jake stood over me and washed me down with his urine. I drank as much as I could but, as I opened my mouth to take it, semen was still running over my lips.'

It was 3 a.m. when I came out of the red-curtained room. I had been overwhelmed by Crystal's story. In the end, she said she had to go. I felt better, so I decided to leave.

The main gaming room was full — red-eyed women hung onto the levers of one armed bandits, tired men stretched themselves against the unyielding backs of their chairs, yawning gamblers tried to disguise their disappointment with their badly drawn cards. I stepped back as a waitress —full breasted with a pert smile and a quick and purposeful walk — strode past me carrying a tray of drinks at head height. Someone was close behind me. I felt the warmth of his body.

I turned.

A man with a patch over his one eye stood in front of me.

'You're not leaving are you?' he said. 'Follow me. You might be able to earn a bit of money. Or, if not, you might be a bit of money!'

I knew exactly what he meant. I licked my lips — they had gone instantly dry. He walked towards a heavy leather-padded door. He opened it and walked in. I could not do anything but follow.

9. THE JOURNEY NORTH
DEGRADATION

I found my pick-up in a high-fenced compound at the back of New York New York. The guard ran his hand across my breasts as he handed me back my keys. I felt my nipples hardening at his touch. He noticed them too and grabbed my arm. He was just pulling me into his tiny smoke-filled office when another man arrived. It was obviously his boss and the guard let me go.

'Clear off, tramp!' shouted the supervisor. 'Go and peddle your services somewhere else.'

My nipples hardened more as I felt a wave of humiliation set off by his words.

I walked quickly to my pick-up. The front nearside was bashed in but, when I turned the key, the growling engine started straight away. Both the front tyres caught on the bent fender as I turned out of the car park, but I reckoned I could manage with that. The guard licked out his tongue as I drove past his hut. I lifted up my T shirt and exposed my breasts to show him what he had missed.

As I drove off into the desert, I felt a strange sense of emptiness. I was going in a circle, I thought — my whole life was going in a circle, and I was getting nowhere. I stared up at the scorching midday sun. I had suffered enough of its heat. I turned away from it and drove north.

Day became night and night became day. Sometimes I drove beneath the stars and slept in the back of the pick-up. Sometimes I drove all day and stayed in a cheap motel. Sometimes I just drove until I was so tired I stopped and fell asleep slumped at the wheel.

One day, bleary eyed from a sleepless night, and picking my way between scrap cars and burned out trailers on the edge of an unnamed and half empty township, my heart started pounding as I caught sight of something in my rear view mirror. I was sure I saw Father Dawson's old black Ford sedan — the prized possession so carefully cleaned and shined by his obedient penitents! My heart leapt as I saw two bright flashing mirrors glittering on the polished black wings but, as quickly as it appeared, it fell back and disappeared. I kept looking in my rear view mirror all morning, but I never saw it again. In the end, I decided it was my imagination — too much sun, I thought, and another good reason to be heading north.

Once, parked in a truck stop on the I80 near the home of Buffalo Bill Cody — North Platte, Nebraska — I was woken by someone pulling at my panties. It was a fat trucker, stinking with engine oil and greasy from days on the road without a wash. I pushed my hands down to stop him, but he brushed them away as if I was a fly. He was heavy and disgusting. He bore down on me as he pushed his weighty cock into my cunt and I could not move — I felt as if I would suffocate.

Another time I met a young thin man who drove a 1958 Pontiac — all chrome and jet age. He tied me face forward across the bonnet during a sudden snow storm, tore down my skirt and panties and whipped me viciously with his leather belt. The cutting lashes burnt me in a way I had never known. Each slashing contact was like a sudden flame across my skin, then, as it subsided, I felt a strange increasing numbness spreading out from the source until my whole body was on fire. I shivered against the cold metal of the car's shiny bonnet and stared out into the blizzard as he stood behind me and thrashed me until he was exhausted. I shivered with cold while, at the same time, I shook with the burning flames of heat that the belt set off. I was giddy and spinning with the mixed sensations, and I jerked with repeated orgasms even after he had stopped and had pulled the belt back around his narrow waist.

I made my way east until one day, almost suddenly, I found myself in a strange and different world. Everything looked odd — it was as though I had jumped back in time. There were timber barns, horses drawing small black tarpaulin-covered traps, and pedestrians in strange clothing — women in long skirts fronted by white aprons with tightly fitting bonnets on their heads, men with black suits and black wide brimmed, low-domed hats. Everywhere there was an ancient slowness, all around something of a time gone by. I was in Amish country, the home of the Anabaptist Christians who settled here from Switzerland in the late seventeenth century. This is a place where tradition rules, where things of the modern world are either forbidden or despised. This is the place where the population refers to the other citizens not in their community as 'English'.

I called at Lehman's, a huge barn filled with old fashioned stoves, wooden tools and ancient kitchen appliances. A bearded youth in a black hat took me aside as I wandered amongst racks of rakes and brooms. I saw his cock stiffening inside his trousers as he spoke. I ran my hand down their front. He pulled me behind the shelving, pushed me onto my knees and drove his dry stiff shaft into my anus. I cried out and he held his hand across my mouth. He was so forceful and urgent, wrapping his arm beneath my hips to give himself enough purchase for his frantic thrusts. His semen was hot as it sprayed up into my rectum. I clenched my buttocks around his cock and sucked it all out. He took his arm from around my waist and I fell forward with my face on the floorboards, gasping for breath and shivering with painful joy. I licked my tongue out and tasted the metallic sting of cleaning fluid — the wooden floor was still wet with its disinfectant dousing. My head reeled with its astringent aroma. I laid my tongue flat against it, desperate to taste its bitter sweetness to the full.

An older man came around the laden shelving and shouted at the youth as he struggled to push his still hard and dripping cock back into his trousers. The man told the youth to get back to work instead of, as he said, 'Carrying out the devil's own work'. The older man looked down and spat on me. I wiped it slowly from my face. He spat again. This time I let it dribble down my cheeks. I rolled onto my back and licked it as it oozed down against the corner of my mouth. He dribbled more spit onto me in disgust. I opened my mouth fully and let it drip straight in. He undid his trousers and held his cock in his hand. I watched the stream of urine pouring down on me. I kept my mouth wide open and licked out my tongue. His urine flowed in a strong golden torrent into my gaping mouth. I closed my eyes in joy as my mouth was filled to overflowing. The salty heat of his urine ran over my chin, into my ears and hair. When the flow stopped, I opened my eyes and swallowed, taking it all down in a single thirst quenching draught. He looked down at me in contempt. I felt dirty and corrupt.

He told some others to take me out.

'Her presence offends the Lord,' he said. 'Do with her as you will. She is a servant of Satan and deserves only our scorn.'

I felt wretched. Their contempt overwhelmed me. I lost all sense of dignity. I felt I could do nothing except let them do with me as they would. I had no reason to resist, no desire for anything but their will and their contempt.

Three men dragged me through the shop. Customers stared at me — bearded men lowering their black domed hats, women clasping their hands together in front of their long blue, apron covered skirts. The reddened cheeks of the women stood out against their white, tight-fitting bonnets. They all shook their heads and looked down at the ground as though the very sight of me was too much to bear.

The men took me out into a yard at the rear. Small black horse-drawn carts were parked in a neat row. The reins of the horses, shackled in their shiny wooden shafts, were wrapped around a long hitching post. Even the horses seemed to turn away from me as I was pulled past on my back, naked except for my panties wound up like a rag around my ankles.

They threw me down in the back of a cart. The horse in the shafts whinnied and the cart shook as the frightened animal clattered its hooves nervously. The men looked down at me as I lay sobbing and distraught, contemptible and humiliated. The cart rocked as each one clambered up in turn.

The first stripped my panties down over my feet and tied them across my mouth. He pulled them so tight that my teeth closed together in front of it. He held his stiff cock tightly in his hand. I watched the end swelling with ever-increasing pressure as his mouth hung slackly and spit dribbled down into his long beard. He sprayed his semen over my eyes and into my hair, then dropped down onto his knees and squeezed out the last drops against my flaring nostrils. The second held a riding crop across my aching nipples as he spurted his semen on the insides of my thighs. It ran down against the soft open flesh of my cunt and mixed with the old man's semen that was still flowing from my anus. The last one turned me over on my face and thrashed me across the buttocks with a short leather belt. He told me how sinful I was, how I was beyond redemption, and how there was nothing that would help me except the pain of punishment.

'And I will deliver the pain of God's vengeance to your evil body,' he ranted. 'I will flail your flesh until you beg forgiveness! It will feel like the lapping flames of hell around your sinful flesh!'

I rose up against the slashing leather and, as the cutting blows increased in strength and pace and, as a massive surge of blinding joy overtook me, I found myself yelling out uncontrollably.

'I am such a sinner! Forgive me! Lord! Please, Lord, forgive me my sins!'

I screeched out so loud I was aware of nothing else. It was unstoppable. I couldn't prevent myself yelping and screaming.

'Lord, forgive me! Lord, forgive me!'

The leather cut across my burning buttocks. They were on fire, and I only wanted more.

'Please, oh, Lord! Please! Help me find redemption!' I cried.

Tears ran from my wide staring eyes, spit dribbled from my gaping mouth. I just needed more. Even though it was too much, it was not enough.

The man threw down the belt and spat on me. I gasped and panted. I felt like an animal. I dropped my chin towards my chest and flared my nostrils. He stepped back and looked at his creation — a wanton animal whose limits and restraints had been completely destroyed. It was as though he had released everything evil inside me that was desperate to get out.

I jumped up and ran out into the open yard. I ducked down and grabbed a handful of mud. I smeared it across my breasts. It felt sticky and cold. I rubbed it around my hard nipples. I scooped up more and plastered it across my thighs. I turned and looked around — dozens of Amish were gathered in a gawping crowd. I bent down and started slurping at the mud and buried my face in it. I ate it. I swallowed it ravenously. I rolled in some more. I opened my legs and showed my naked cunt to everyone. I wanted to be completely shamed. I wanted them to urinate on me. I wanted to be dirtied. I wanted to be disgraced and shamed. I wanted to be buried in humiliating sinfulness.

In the end, I dropped back exhausted. No one spoke. Everyone slowly shuffled away. I felt the heat of my cunt. It spread into my whole body. I was on fire with it. Suddenly it exploded. Like a bursting star in my mind, my joy ignited me from within. I was filled with it. I jerked. I went rigid. I was completely overtaken. My body went stiff. I tried to cry out but could not. Then as suddenly as it had come, it released in me a massive surging orgasm, and I fell back to the muddy ground, utterly depleted.

I lay on the ground and realised that I still wanted more. I wanted to be shackled in place of one of the horses. I wanted to be driven cruelly from field to field, pulling the heavy cart, carrying out only my master's wishes. I wanted to be fed from a bag and made to drink from dirty ponds. I wanted to be thrashed on my buttocks when I failed to keep the proper pace. I wanted to be pulled harshly by the bit between my teeth if I was too slow. I wanted to be left in the shafts overnight so that, even before the dawn, tired and exhausted, I was ready again to do my master's bidding.

A few men lifted me up and flung me into the back of a cart. I lay there, semen dripping from my face and between my legs as I shivered again and again with the gradually ebbing jerks of my delightful and repeated orgasms. One of them threw my clothes down on top of me as they walked back into the store. A child ran up and threw some clods of mud at me. They stuck to my still jerking body. I felt completely disgusting.

The cart was driven out of the town and I was thrown down into a water-filled ditch. They ordered me to wash myself and watched until I had finished. They told me they never wanted to see my face again and drove off.

I lay in the ditch trembling with fear until it was dark. In the end, I plucked up enough courage to creep back into the town. I found the pick-up still parked in front of Lehman's. The keys were still in it. It had been daubed with graffiti. I felt eyes on me as I drove away, filled with the deepest sense of shame and yet, at the same time, uncontrollably excited by my humiliation.

I was worn out by the time I finally drove into Cleveland. My experiences with the Amish still filled my mind. I ached with the thought of the humiliation they had showered on me. The sense of shame I had felt at their hands had infected me with a desire for more even. I knew now that my own salvation — if it was ever possible — would ultimately only come hand in hand with my complete submission to degradation and disgrace. I knew that I craved only more shame, more ill-treatment, and that I would not even be able to go on until at least some of that need had been satisfied.

I booked into the first place I saw — 'Frankie's Downtown Motel'. I slept all afternoon, naked on top of the small soft bed. When I woke I was hungry. I was told there was a good place to eat near the main university square. I quickly got lost and found myself walking around the near deserted streets. I walked onto the corner of Lorain and West 53rd and the whole scene changed. Suddenly I was confronted by the smell of beer and sweat, by clusters of people huddled in dark corners, and by brightly dressed women bending to the open windows of cars cruising on side lights. I had walked straight into the red light district.

I got talking to a young girl, Rosalind. She had been a prostitute for a year and was, she said, 'quite experienced compared to some'.

She was waiting for one of her regulars and, she said, if I wanted I could join her. He was a good looking man of about thirty five, she said, a Russian, she thought, and, importantly, with plenty of cash to spare. A few minutes later, he drew up in a chauffeur driven black Mercedes. Rosalind said he was going to have to pay a fair bit extra for both of us — even if I was new at the game — but, she promised him, it would be well worth it. He smiled and invited us both to get into the cavernous leather covered interior of the limousine.

It started straightaway. To begin with, I watched. Rosalind knelt on the floor of the limo and unzipped the young man's trousers. He had a big cock — thick and venous with a swollen heavy glans. She took it into her mouth slowly, dribbling her spit around the head then turning her mouth sideways to it and licking its length to ensure its wetness.

He turned to me and stared.

'We'll stop somewhere and see if you can cut it as a whore,' he said, casually.

Rosalind looked at me and raised her eyebrows. I could already feel the heat of my cunt.

We came to a busy truck stop on the I89. He opened the door of the limousine and pushed me out.

'Go on, bitch. Let's see some action.'

He motioned me away with his hand as the rear window slowly slid up.

The place was full of truck drivers and bikers. Some women dressed in black leather played pool. I got into conversation with some men at the rowdy bar. They kept buying me drinks — 'Another Bud for the lady,' the fattest one, who seemed to have more money than the others, kept saying as soon as my glass was half empty. I soon felt really drunk — I could hear my slurred words, and when I moved, things moved in the opposite direction. They were all hands, every one of them grabbing at me whenever they got a chance. They talked about what a woman would or would not do for money. It was great fun. I said I would suck any cock for $20, and fuck for $80. I didn't charge extra for anal, I said, because I liked it too much, but if they wanted to whip me that would cost them $100 — 'just for the pain'.

I felt like a slut, offering myself to these smelly, fat, bikers and truck drivers. And the sense of disgust that came over me as I realised this excited me as much as anything could. Yes, it was the revulsion I felt for my own degradation that brewed up a fire of excitement inside me. It was irresistible. I got up on a table and started dancing. It was incredible to have all their eyes fixed on my every movement. Slowly, I removed my T shirt. They all cheered and shouted loudly. Some of them threw the contents of their glasses at me. The hoppy beer ran over my breasts and dripped from my nipples. I squirmed against it. I felt as though I was being showered with urine. It was delectable.

'And you can pee over me for $50!' I shouted out to them.

I wriggled my jeans down onto my hips. My panties were twisted up in the material and they tugged at the flesh of my cunt. I squirmed on it — feeling it pulling apart the swollen edges of my slit, exposing the wet crack at its centre, drawing out its passion only thrilled me more. I pulled against it to increase the tension. It hurt. I pulled against it more. I gulped and felt spit running out between my lips.

I dropped my jeans to the floor and stepped out of them. My panties had pulled down to my knees before disentangling themselves from my jeans. I left them there.

I raised my hands in the air and breathed in deeply.

'But the first one's free! Anything you like!'

I felt completely abandoned to whatever was going to happen — nothing was restraining me.

Several men reached up and lifted me down from the table. I fell backwards into their dirty grasping hands. They held my breasts, pinched my nipples and probed their fingers between my buttocks and into the flesh of my cunt. It all felt delightful! The more they handled me, the more they pinched and poked, the more I smelled their greasy hands and beer-scented breath, the more I was consumed by the delights that were overwhelming me. It was like falling into a delectable and slimy pit.

A huge fat man came forward out of the crowd — even fatter than the one with all the money. Everyone shouted and jeered as he took off his denim shirt and pulled down his jeans. The others held me as the table was pulled aside. The fat man lay down on the floor wearing only his Stars and Stripes boxer shorts. He rolled onto his back like a gigantic whale.

They carried me to him, ordered me to kneel by his side and remove his shorts.

I did as I was told. He was enormous. I could hardly reach over him — his fat belly dished in like a water bed as I bent across him. The hairs on his chest covered two pulpy breasts. His neck was massive, so thick it was impossible to tell where it started or ended. His huge spongy arms flopped by his sides. They were completely covered in tattoos that ran up to a sudden stop above his undefined biceps. He had a short goatee beard and two large silver rings through his left nostril. Another silver ring hung down from his left eyelid. A flying eagle was tattooed on his forehead and both his cheeks were scarred with ugly white slashes.

'With your teeth!' someone shouted. 'With your teeth!'

I bent my head to the leg of his shorts. They smelled rank. I took the hem between my teeth and started to pull them down. I felt deeply humiliated. I tugged hard, but they would not peel away from his fleshy, quivering belly.

One of them slapped me on the bottom. It was sudden and sharp and I pulled back. I knew I shouldn't, but I couldn't help myself. Another smack landed quickly, this time harder and more forceful. I knew it was an instruction to carry on. I did not question it, or look to see who was delivering it. I gripped the material of the shorts as tightly as I could and pulled with all the strength I could muster.

They all jeered at my efforts — chanting rhythmically as I fought desperately to avoid another painful smack. But again it was not good enough. My buttocks clenched as a leather belt cut sharply across them, I winced and my whole body tightened, but I kept at the task that I had been set.

Slowly, the gaudy shorts began to come down. Another slashing stroke with the belt and I fell forward, the shorts still between my teeth but now half way down the bulging white thighs of the fat man on the floor.

His cock and testicles were fully exposed. They hung against his left thigh — flaccid and huge.

Cheers filled the room. Beer sloshed down my back and into my hair.

'Make it hard, whore! Make it hard! Let's see if you're worth the money!'

I took it in my mouth. The foreskin was stretched only loosely over the huge glans beneath. I took the skin into my mouth, teasing it with my tongue, sucking at it. It started straightaway. I felt the glans beginning to throb and soon I tasted its nakedness as it pushed out and began filling my mouth. I put my hand on the shaft and it strengthened under my tightening fingers — thickening at first then lengthening as it filled. I ran my tongue around it and, as I pushed my head down onto it and pulled back, I spread it copiously with my frothing silky spit.

They pulled me off it when it was fully extended. Now I saw how huge it was. It stood vertical and was laced with heavy pulsating veins. The purple engorged glans throbbed rhythmically as it continued to draw the shaft to greater length and thickness.

They held me above it with my legs apart and they cheered as I was lowered down. I felt its heat first, before it touched my skin, then when it touched me I flinched as if I was being burned. Its tip was massive — scalding. They pressed my anus against it. I could not keep my eyes open. I breathed in gulps. I was sweating. I felt dizzy. The pressure was enormous. They pushed me down more. It went in. I felt as if I was being torn apart. Its heat was unbearable. It went in further. It began to fill my innards. I didn't think it would stop. I gasped. I went so hot. I shivered. I broke out in a sweat. I bit my lips. It did no good. I bit my tongue. I could hardly feel the pain.

I had never felt so full. I had never believed I could be so stuffed. I could not stop gasping. Then, at last, it stopped going in. They held me there. I did not dare move — I could not bear even to think of moving. Then, holding me under the armpits and by the ankles they began to rotate me on the massive cock that was buried so deeply into my plugged rectum.

Slowly they turned me on it. I could not believe what was happening. It was unbelievable. I felt as if I was on a spit. The sensation overcame me — the venous shaft pulling around the stretched edges of my anus as it rotated. I thought I was going to pass out. I could not move my body myself — I was fully under their control, completely at their mercy. I shivered with fear as I thought they might drop me onto it.

They took me in one full circle, then another, and another. My head flopped forward and spit ran from my mouth in a stream. They took me around again. The pain in my anus and the feeling of fullness mixed together with my shame and humiliation. As I was taken around again, I knew that my degradation was complete, and with that realisation came the building flood of my orgasm as it gripped me and made me scream out for more. I couldn't believe it — I was suffering more than I had ever suffered, and I was screaming out for more! I was terrified that they might release me and let me drop onto his massive cock, and I was screaming out for more!

I did not know what would happen when I felt the shaft inside my rectum thickening with a surge of semen. I just hung there — screeching, pleading for it, and yet fearing every moment to come. A sudden sweat broke out on my face as I did at last feel it thickening. The pain was sharp at first then it became dull and throbbing as I felt the massive stream of hot semen explode inside me. My whole body jerked with its pulses. I felt it would come up my throat. I opened my mouth and yelped as loud as I could.

The next thing I knew they pulled me off him. I collapsed in their arms as my anal muscle released the still pulsating cock. I was filled with a surge of searing pain. I don't know where it was — it was everywhere. I felt his semen running down the insides of my thighs. I jerked again. My orgasm was unstoppable.

Outside, they took turns to thrash me with their belts. Then they daubed me with grease and dragged me on the muddy ground by a rope wrapped around my ankles. Still I felt the jerking delight of my orgasm. No matter what they did to me, no matter how humiliated I was, my throbbing pleasure only grew. I did not know how it would end. I did not care.

When they were tired of me, they sprayed me with strong smelling detergent then washed me down roughly with a powerful hose. They left me in the car park shivering, wet and dirty, and still jerking rhythmically with the orgasms that continued to throb repeatedly within my pain-racked body. Dollar bills floated down around me as slowly the men made their way back inside.

I opened my eyes. I could barely focus but, in the flickering lights of trucks and bikes, I saw the black Mercedes — the rear window was just going up. The young man inside was nodding with approval. He tossed a thick envelope onto the ground and, as the car pulled away, I saw Rosalind quickly turn and wave.

10. VIRGINIA
JOHNSON'S FARM

I headed towards West Virginia — it seemed right. The glove box was stuffed with money — I could hardly close it!

I felt the moisture from my cunt sticking to the shiny bench seat of the pick-up. When I moved, the soft flesh clung to the plastic surface — it was sore, very sore. My anus was burning — and it would not stop. As I lifted myself off the seat it was like having a scorching flame rammed inside me. I felt so mixed up. I felt disgusted with myself — I knew I had allowed myself to be degraded like never before — but I also knew that very degradation had satisfied me in ways that nothing else could. I felt so ashamed of myself but, even as I felt the shame, a wave of pleasure flooded through me. I had always known of my need for humiliation, but now I had explored it further than ever before, and I had found out that true pleasure could only come from inhabiting its depths. I knew my life would never be the same again — from now on there was only one direction from which my joy would come, and I must pursue it — in every form, in any way it was offered, or forced onto me, I must pursue it. From now on, no master could be too cruel, no punishment could be too severe, and no humiliation could debase me too much. No matter how much I yelled for liberation, no matter how much I begged for release, I knew I could no longer be rescued from my need for more punishment and the squalid filth of degradation that I craved so much. I knew there would be an end to my journey, but now I knew that my travels would end only when I was faced with the pleasure of the ultimate, overwhelming disgrace. For the moment, I thought, that could wait.

I drove along the Blue Ridge Parkway — five hundred miles of National Park created around a strip of road running south west to north east up the Appalachian Mountains. It was perfect peace — 45 miles per hour maximum speed, no one else on the road, and crystal clear views of pristine forests set against gently sloping rocky mountain tops.

I stopped at Peaks of Otter. I sat on my ground floor balcony watching a huge red sun dip between the valley's gentle cleft cut above a clearing on the opposite side of the placid lake.

The sun set quickly and I watched the full moon slowly rising in its place. I stared at the stars — it was magical. The next thing I knew, I awoke, shivering cold — it was 3am!

The next morning I went for breakfast in the hotel. It was fussy and full of outdoor types and young families weekending away from Washington DC. A few attending fathers couldn't resist ogling me when I walked into the breakfast room. I smiled at each one. If any of them had offered me his cock, I would have taken it.

I picked up a trail guide from the shop. I thought a day walking in the woods would do me good. I needed a break and this seemed the perfect place to take it.

'Don't get lost now,' said the woman as she tided her counter. She was dressed in old fashioned clothes, a black skirt with a white apron and a white bonnet. 'There's nobody about though. It should be good and quiet.'

I followed the trail signs to Johnson's Farm. The woods were beautiful — heavy-leafed red maple and dappled yellow ash created magical bowers around every turn. A clear stream trickled along the path — it was delightful. I lay down beside it and stared up into the canopy of leaves. I closed my eyes, felt my cunt and listened to the sound of the babbling water. I must have fallen asleep because the next thing I knew was opening my eyes and realising that the light was fading. I scrambled up and quickly decided that the farm was probably nearer than the hotel. Walking hurriedly, still slightly dazed with sleep, I went on.

At the top of the steep rise I finally came out at Johnson's Farm — a neat white clapboarded house with a surrounding white fence, a wood store, an implement shed and a small stable. The area around it had been cleared of trees and had become a naturalised meadow of grass and flowers. I smelled the hay and poppies. It made me giddy.

I walked to the implement store. A large, heavy, harrowing device constructed to be drawn by a horse sat beside it. A metal seat was planted amongst the labyrinth of steelwork that formed the carcass of the machine, and two footplates rested above the rods and spikes that twisted around them.

A tall muscular man in black, high belted trousers and a white collarless shirt raked hay on the far side of the house. Under the wide shady porch roof, a woman worked on a wooden tub of washing. I stood by the strange farm implement. I was unsure whether to approach the man or woman, they both looked busy and I thought they might be intolerant of an interruption to their chores.

Suddenly, I shivered with cold. I heard a movement behind me. I turned. A beautiful young woman was walking through the meadow grass. She wore an open-necked white cotton smock pulled tight at her narrow waist. Her hair was red, her lips full, and her skin perfectly smooth. The tousled ends of her flaming hair gently caressed her shoulders. She smiled broadly — her teeth were large and white. She was truly beautiful.

'My name's May. Those are my foster parents — the Johnsons. I was an orphan and they took me in. She needed someone to help with the chores, he wanted someone for his own pleasure. He'll be over in a while. If you stay, you'll see how he gets his pleasure — and how he makes his money. They'd never be able to keep this place going if it wasn't for me. What's your name?'

'Syra.'

'That's a nice name. Syra, I have a boyfriend, his name's Jesse. He's going to take me away from here. He lives in Roanoke. He's coming tonight. But old man Johnson says he wants me here, and I know what that means. Syra, it'll be dark soon, and when it's dark here, you can't see a thing. Hey, I've got an idea — a great idea. You could stay here and pretend to be me. What do you think? He'll never know, his mind's on other things anyway. Just do as he tells you and he won't know the difference. For me, Syra, would you do that for me? It would save my life. I promise. It would save my life. I would be eternally grateful. I would not forget you. Ever. Will you, Syra? Will you?'

I couldn't believe what was happening. In a couple of minutes I had been asked to stand in for someone I didn't know, someone I didn't even look like, to do something that hadn't been explained to me, for a reason that I didn't understand. I started to think of questions but, as I began to sort them out, they all disappeared from my mind.

'Yes, I'll do it.'

I couldn't believe what I had said. It was a weird moment of madness, and I couldn't hold it back — it was as though some strange force was compelling me.

'Syra! That's marvellous! I'll show you. Look, take your workwear off. You must wear my dress. Then you'll look like a girl. It will look pretty on you. Here.'

'But my hair? Look the moon's coming up. It'll be obvious it's not you.'

'It doesn't matter. I promise. Quickly! We must hurry.'

She wriggled her white dress of her shoulders, slackened the belt and let it drop to the ground at her feet. She stood there for a moment, the setting sun catching the highlights of her red hair, her glowing nakedness set off by a precise triangle of red pubic hair. It was as though she and the setting sun were one. I pulled my jeans and T shirt off. I threw my panties on top of them. She ran over, grabbed them and pulled them on.

'This will be a fine disguise. Syra, quick, put my dress on. Syra! You have no pubic hair! No matter. No matter.'

The dress fitted perfectly. It was still warm from her body, and it smelled sweet, like the meadow grass and flowers which surrounded us. I suddenly felt embarrassed that she was wearing my dirty panties.

'Here. Syra. Come over here. This is the harrow. It hasn't been used on the fields for years; most of them are overgrown anyway. Here, climb up, before he comes over. Climb up!'

I didn't know what I was doing but I did as she said. Her sense of urgency was overpowering and the mystery of it all had sucked me in.

I held onto the side bars of the harrow. There was a small step up to the seat which was wide with a raised ridge at the front that flattened out and widened towards the rear. It was mounted on a long, wide, single spring. Beneath it were two heavy footrests made of metal, set about shoulder width apart. Behind them were another two metal footrests set closer together.

'Yes, get up. It's easy. Here, sit on the seat. It's adjustable. You'll see.'

I sat down on the metal seat. The dress rose up and my bare skin touched the cold metal. It made me shiver.

'It's always like that to start with, but it gets warmer.'

She laughed and hurriedly came up beside me. It seemed that now she had hardly any time at all.

I settled my bottom against the broad perforated metal seat. The raised centre at the front pressed into the crack of my cunt. I felt the flesh opening under the pressure. I felt another shiver — this time of delight.

'Yes, hitch your dress up. He'll ask you to do that anyway, so you may as well do it now. That's right. Pull it up to your waist. Now, place your feet on those two footrests at the front. That's right. Now, if you want, you can hold onto the handles that they used to use to control this thing. Look, like this.'

She took my hands and placed them onto two long handles that stood up from the spikes and tines of the implement. The grips were worn and shiny from years of use. I wrapped my fingers around them.

'That's it, Syra. You've got it. Now, just wait a few minutes, until the sun has gone down and he'll be over — old man Johnson. Don't worry about him. He'll tell you exactly what to do, no worry. Oh! I forgot! The bonnet! Here, put the bonnet on. See? I told you, he'll never know the difference! And it suits you!'

She was very excited as she pulled a white bonnet onto

my head. She secured it with a bow beneath my chin with two material cords that dangled from its front corners.

'Perfect! That's just perfect. Syra, I'm so grateful. I can't tell you how much. Syra, really, you've saved my life. Bless you, Syra. Bless you. I won't forget you. I promise. I won't ever forget you.'

She got down from the harrow and silently backed away into the woods. I saw the flash of her pale skin in the growing blueness of the moonlight then, like a phantom, she was gone.

Suddenly, I felt alone. I shivered again. It had gone really cold.

I looked across the meadow — everything was silver and blue in the moonlight. Old man Johnson was walking towards me. I hung my head so that the frilly peak of the bonnet partially obscured my face. He nodded as he walked past his wife. She emptied the washing tub over the edge of the porch, picked up her washing and went into the house. He rested the fork that he was carrying against the store shed.

'Well, May, I'm pleased to see you are waiting. It's an improvement. Perhaps you've got all these dangerous ideas you've been having out of your head at last. I hope so.'

I didn't dare speak. My heart was thumping — I could feel it in my throat. I tried to swallow, but my mouth was too dry.

He reached into the store shed and took hold of some shiny black leather reins. He dangled them in his hands as, nodding his head slowly in thought, he walked around the harrow.

'I think extra tight tonight, May. I've let you off too

easily lately. Discipline is what you need. Yes, more discipline will rid you of these wild ideas you have of boys and running away. Now, make yourself ready. What are you thinking of? Off the seat! Off the seat!'

I wasn't sure what he meant, but his angry voice revealed his mood, and I could tell he would not tolerate any mistakes. I stood up on the footrests and lifted my bottom off the seat.

'Too slow! Don't be so slow! Hitch up your skirt properly. Hitch it up!'

He leant over the side of the harrow and began binding one of the shiny black leather reins around my right foot. He pulled it tight, securing my foot firmly to the footrest. The strap cut into my skin and, when I tried to move my foot, I could barely wriggle my toes. He tied the other one in the same way. I felt unsteady as I tried to keep standing and I loosened my grip on the handles.

His anger was instant.

'May! May! I will not tolerate disobedience!'

I felt a sudden pain across my buttocks as he lashed them viciously with the remaining reins. I was jolted forwards — as much by the shock as the pain — and, to steady myself, tightened my grip on the handles.

He wound a leather strap around each hand and bound them tightly to the shiny handles. I stood on the footrests, crouching, barely upright, still with my head hung for fear of being recognised. I was gasping loudly, filled with fear, and boiling with expectation.

He turned a small metal wheel in front of me and a metal bar rose up in front of my face. The red paint that covered it had been scraped off in the centre.

'May! Do not make me wait any more! Take the bar. It is nearly time. Take the bar!'

Another burning pain cut across my buttocks as he brought the spare reins down sharply. This time I knew for certain what he meant. It was obvious that the scrapes in the red paint on the bar were teeth marks!

I bent my head down and took the metal bar between my teeth. I couldn't bite down, it was too hard, but I closed my lips around it and held it nevertheless. Straight away I felt totally captive — with my feet, hands and head held firmly against the heavy steel harrow, I could no longer move at all. It was as if I was part of the heavy device — I was as solid and fixed as it was.

'Now, May, tonight I will be watching with even more care than usual. I will be looking very carefully indeed. And this time, you will feel the full sting of my hand if you do not please me.'

I heard him move back, then nothing. I waited for him to speak, but he was silent. I waited for a blow across my buttocks, but no blow came. I looked up nervously under the peak of the bonnet. The meadow was empty and soundless — no chirping cricket, no hooting owl, no rustling leaf. It was as though the whole world was completely still.

I kept my mouth around the bar, and my heart was still beating fast but, in a strange way, I almost began to relax. Then, suddenly, I heard the sound of footsteps behind me. It couldn't be old man Johnson, he had moved to the side and I had not heard him move again. Yes, he must still be there, watching as he said he would. No, this was someone else! Someone was creeping up behind me! A twig cracked, then silence again, but it was only for a second, as a sudden metallic creak told me that someone was climbing up onto the back of the harrow.

The harrow itself did not move, it was too heavy and

solid, but I knew there was someone there — I felt a presence. I shivered with cold.

A finger glanced my buttocks. I knew it was a finger, I could feel the warmth of its tip and the cutting sharpness of its nail. It traced a line around my taut left buttock, slowly at first then quicker. Then it stopped, as though he was looking at me, planning his next move. Then the finger traced around my other buttock. It was just the same as before, slow at first then quicker. But this time, he dug his nail in deeper. Then he pinched my skin, and I felt his thumbnail as well, and I bit a little harder against the metal bar. Its hardness hurt. I let it go straight away, releasing it from my mouth and gasping out, as much in response to the sudden unexpected pain of his pinch, as to the harsh pain caused by the pressure on my teeth.

There was silence for a moment, then a movement at the side told me that old man Johnson was alongside. I felt the cutting smack of the leather reins in his hand as he brought them down hard on my bottom. I threw my head back in a reflex response to the pain.

'Take the bar!' he ordered. 'Take it and keep it in your mouth! You know better than to let it go — and when there is hardly any pain to bear. May! What is the matter with you! Have you learned nothing from your training? Take the bar! Take it!'

I dropped my head and put my mouth around the bar again. It was so hard against my teeth, and I could not keep it away from them. I gripped it as well as I could. The corners of my mouth were pressed in hard by the bar but I could do nothing to stop my teeth from making contact with the harsh metal. I tasted the creamy sharpness of the red paint. I closed my lips together again and waited.

I felt the tracing finger again. This time, it ran along

the crack between my buttocks, from the near flat valley of the bottom of my back to the open wet slit of my cunt. It stopped there for a moment, then pressed between them and opened them out. I felt the cool night air against my anus and the exposed flesh of my cunt. I knew he was looking at me, analysing me, deciding what to do with me. I felt my anus dilate a little and I tightened my buttocks in the hope that he would not notice. He prised my buttocks open more. He obviously had noticed. I could not stop it, my anus, I felt it opening more. I could not stop it inviting his interest.

He circled his nail around its edge, once stopping and pressing it in before continuing. I found his attention irresistible — I could not hold back my arousal. I felt the ring of my anus heating, opening, relaxing. He stopped circling the edge and pressed instead against the centre. I offered no resistance — his finger went straight in. I bit hard onto the bar in my mouth — I did not care about the pain that was transmitted into my gums. I opened my eyes wide. His finger went in further, and it did not stop. I swallowed and that made me bite even harder onto the bar. My teeth ground against it — I heard them and I felt the extra pain that was now penetrating my ears and neck.

I felt his knuckle against my anus; his finger was in as deep as it would go. He pressed against it, increasing the pressure but no longer able to get it in any further. He waited, not moving. I felt my anus throbbing. I felt it tightening then relaxing. I felt it pulsating and burning. I bit down harder against the bar. I felt more pain — now it was in my neck and chest. Then, suddenly, he pulled his finger out. I felt the ring of my anus trying to hold it in. It tightened under the pressure of withdrawal, tugging at the intruding finger, now wanting it to stay there forever, but it could not hold it. I did not bring my buttocks together in relief; instead, I opened them more with a sense of excited dissipation.

I felt empty when his finger came out. I felt the gaping hole of my anus. I felt the heat and the cold, and I bit down harder on the bar and the pain in my mouth filled me with a need for anything he wanted to do to me. I did not care what it was — I just wanted it. More than anything, I wanted what he decided I should have.

I knew it was his cock — it was so hot. It burned the edges of my anus — just its touch burned me. As it started to go in, I realised how big it was, how solid, how weighty. It was wet — he must have spit on it — and it slipped in so easily. He paused for a moment, just to let me experience the heat of it perhaps, then he pressed again and it continued to penetrate me. It seemed to last forever — it was as though its progress into me would go on until the end of time. I was filled before it stopped. I felt full in my throat. It was as though my whole body was filled with it, and still he was forcing it in — still there was more to come.

I crouched there, bound by the tight leather reins, unable to move — not wanting to move — my teeth clenched forcefully around the unforgiving steel bar, filled to the brim by his heavy, massive cock. When finally it stopped, I felt as if its throbbing head was in my chest. My rectum was completely filled by it. Then it drew back. It tugged at my innards and I felt its full fire, and I closed my eyes and tightened my clenching teeth, and I felt spit running into the back of my nose. I flared my nostrils and breathed heavily and the spit ran down them and dribbled over my top lip. It ran around my wide-stretched mouth then, in a bubbling river, streamed down onto my chin.

And he pushed it back in and, as it reached the top, again it pulled back. And he set up a slow rhythm — in and out, in and out. I breathed in time with its beat. The flow of spit down my nostrils increased as his cock went in, and decreased as it pulled back. I felt part of the massive harrow — as solid and unmovable as it was. I was a tool, an implement — only there for the huge cock, for its pleasure, its need, its fertilizing seed.

There was no warning; its semen came suddenly, like lava from an exploding volcano. I open my eyes wide. I did not know what would happen. I felt the scalding liquid running inside of me, unable to escape. I was filled with fear. I was plugged too tight to take it all. Only when he pulled the cock free did it run out. And it flowed copiously, streaming down the insides of my thighs, over the backs of my knees, down my calves and onto my tightly bound feet. I closed my eyes in relief, but my body stayed as fixed as it had been since I was bound by my hands and feet to the unyielding harrow.

And it was not over. I did not have to wait long for the next. He did the same — filled my anus brimful with his semen. The next one took my cunt, the next, both. I don't know when my orgasms started — I think it was when it started to rain and I felt its cool droplets washing the semen from my feet. But even when they did start, I could not let them out — I was too solidly fixed — I just absorbed them all, one after another. I bit on the steel bar so hard that my teeth ground loudly. I opened my eyes as wide as they would open — I thought they would explode. The frantic jerking that was set off by my released joy happened inside me, it joined with the running semen and the stuffing cocks and, crammed with it all, I descended into a pleasure from which I thought it impossible to return. And then it went black and, as cold and heat mixed together like heaven and hell, I felt no more.

I walked back down to the twisting track in a daze. The moonlight had faded and the sun was already coming up by the time I got back to the motel. Everything was bathed in purple, gold and red. I shivered in the chill of the morning air. I went to my room and dropped straight to sleep. I dreamt of the night before, seeing images of myself, bound to the harrow being taken one after another by unseen men who had come throughout the night to have their pleasure.

I woke with a start. I jumped up and ran across to the motel. I was barely in time for breakfast. I gobbled it quickly and went into the shop to tell the woman there about what had happened. She was not there.

'Oh, where's the lady who was here yesterday?' I asked.

'I don't know, sweetie. The shop was closed all day yesterday. I had to take my old daddy to hospital.'

'But I spoke to a lady here yesterday, after breakfast. She gave me a trail guide. I went to Johnson's Farm.'

'Johnson's Farm! Now that's a joke. You couldn't get through to Johnson's Farm nowadays, even with a chainsaw. Nobody's even seen the place for years.'

'But I was there yesterday! I was with their foster daughter, May.'

'You're a fine joker that's for sure. Johnson's Farm! May! She must have been dead for 70 years. Ran away with a ploughman called Jesse from Roanoke. They escaped on a train. She was dressed as a boy, they say. And old Johnson and his wife? He was supposed to have been a cruel man, that's for sure, but when they found what he'd done to his wife they lynched him the same day. They must have been dead nearly a 100 years. Wow! Lady, I don't know where you've been, or what you've been doing, but it ain't been at the Johnson's farm, and it ain't been with May Johnson. Not unless it was her ghost!'

I shivered all over as a fresh coldness spread across my skin. I reached around and felt my buttocks — they were sore. I bit my teeth together and I could still feel the pain from the harsh steel bar. I didn't care what she was telling me, I knew what had happened, ghost or not, I knew what had happened. Suddenly, the scent of new mown hay came into my nostrils and, as I turned and caught my reflection in a mirror, I saw I was still wearing the white cotton smock!

11. PRESQUE ISLE
BLINDFOLDED

It was hot, too hot for the season, too hot for my clothes — I was soaked with sweat. I had driven off the I90 to get a break and found myself on the shores of Lake Erie in the Presque Isle National Park. A tall ranger had given me a map and pointed out a good place to park.

'You're the second stranger today, Ma'am. It's unusual for the time of year, to see so many outsiders, quite unusual.'

I sat back on a broad wooden bench and stared out across a grassy meadow enclosed by tall birch trees. They shimmered in the warm wind that blew across the vast expanses of water contained in the Great Lakes of North America. It was a good place to be.

Two young women in bikinis lay side by side on the grass. Their lightly tanned and shapely forms were dappled with the flickering light beneath the canopy of trees. My eyes roved over their slim taut bodies. Their stomachs were flat and, where they dished down between their hips, the material at the front of their bikini bottoms was raised slightly from their smooth skin. I knew that if I was close enough, and at the correct angle, I would be able to see beneath the material to the tops of their cracks.

I got up, went closer and lay down not far away from them. I pretended I was lying casually on the grass to feel the warmth of the sun. I felt a bit silly. I did not have a bra on, and I did not know how people around here felt about being topless, so I kept my T shirt on. I pushed my hands down the front of my jeans and pulled my panties up tightly against my cunt — the light pink material tugged into the crack of my flesh, and I felt the delightful tension it caused against its raised edges. I pulled them up a bit more — it was delectable.

One of the young women lifted her knees. The taut material of her bikini bottoms stretched tighter between her raised hips. I knelt down and stared. I allowed myself to imagine what lay in the dark shadow along the gusset of the yellow flower-patterned bikini bottoms. I thought of the smooth skin of her stomach. In my mind, I followed it down to the slow, curved incline that rose upwards to the top of her crack. I could almost smell the fragrance of her slit. I pictured the delightful split of flesh, the neat valley that lay between the swollen edges, the softness, the nakedness, the sticky wetness that gleamed at its centre.

I imagined myself bending down to it, pulling away the covering of the bright yellow bikini bottoms. I felt the tension of my own panties against the flesh of my cunt as I leant forward more. I thought of how her bikini bottoms would come down to just above her knees, how she would raise her hips with excitement from the exposure, how she would lift up her flesh and, sensing the wetness along it even more as the hot sun heated its surface, how she would allow her delectable crack to open. I saw myself place my head between her thighs. I imagined their heat against my ears. I saw my tongue licking out — wet and glistening with spit. I saw it probing towards that beautiful slit, reaching out for it, its own pinkness seeking out the pinkness of the shimmering soft and fragrant crack.

Yes, that was all I could think of — bending over her, straddling her head with my knees, raising my bottom high, as I dropped my lips down against that perfect, naked, exposed slit. I could almost taste it — sweet scented and aromatic. I wanted to smother myself in it. I could feel my nostrils flaring to take more of her wetness against my nose. I would sniff at her. I would breathe her in as deeply as I could. I would inhale her; let her delightful scent into every cell of my body. I would feel her essence inside me before, finally, I would allow my tongue to make contact. I would hold it back as long as I possibly could — delighting in the anticipation — but in the end, I would not be able to restrain myself and, as my outstretched tongue touched the soft flesh that beckoned it, I would open my mouth and press my lips against it. Then I would give way. I would slobber on it greedily. I would not have the control to please her — I would be unable to tantalise her, unable to satisfy her with any delicacy. I would be ravenous. I would eat at her flesh. Hungry and needy. I would suck at its sloppiness, drink it, consume it until my body lost control completely and I felt the irrepressible jerks of my frenzied orgasm.

I sat up. My hand was between my thighs and my fingers were deep inside my cunt. The two women were staring at me! I felt my face redden. I looked beyond them — youths were playing with a ball, a pair of lovers stroked each other's hair, mothers sat in a group talking, several cars were parked on the grass — one was a big shiny black sedan.

The woman with the yellow bikini smiled. She waved her hand for me to go over. I took my fingers from my cunt —they were wet. I felt my face flush again. I felt ridiculous — discovered, exposed, deeply embarrassed.

'Here, sit with us. I'm Petra, this is Robin,' she said, as I got close to them.

'Hi,' I said, still trembling with excitement, and hiding my wet fingers behind my back. 'I'm Syra.'

Robin sat up and smiled. They were both beautiful.

I sat down, pulled my knees up and wrapped my arms around them. My cunt was still wet and I knew there would be a wet patch on the gusset of my panties. I tightened my buttocks and a wave of delight spread up between them. I slackened my arms a little and let my knees drop slightly apart. Yes, there was a wet patch. I felt another thrill of excitement as I caught Petra staring at it.

'Would you like to play a game?' she asked. 'This is a good place. Look, everybody's enjoying themselves. What do you think?'

'Yes, sure. Why not?'

'Why not indeed,' Petra giggled, obviously amused by my accent. 'Let's play "Blindfold". It's our favourite. Look, we have the blindfold with us, we always have it with us, don't we Robin.'

'We sure do,' said Robin pulling out a black satin scarf from a picnic bag at her side.

'Look, Robin will put the blindfold on you. She'll make it nice and tight. You don't mind that do you?'

I shook my head.

'No, I suppose not.'

Robin knelt by me and placed the black scarf across my eyes. It felt smooth and cool. She pulled it tight and tied it behind me head. I couldn't open my eyes and everything was completely black. For a second, I felt panicky — the scarf was pressing against my eyeballs — and it was claustrophobic not being able to open my eyes — but I took a couple of deep breaths and my fear eased.

'Don't worry, Syra. You'll soon get into the swing of it.'

I felt Petra's hand on my shoulder. It was warm and soft. She ran her fingers around it. I lifted my arm slightly so that she could feel where she wanted. Circling her fingers lightly, she caressed the smooth cup of my armpit — it tickled and I giggled.

She pulled away.

'Right-ho,' she said mimicking an English accent. 'Let's begin. Stand up, Syra. Upright! Stand to attention!'

I pushed my arms down by my sides, turned my fingers up against the base of my palms and pushed my thumbs down straight so that they reached beyond the first knuckle of my forefingers.

'Good,' said Petra. 'Very good.'

I stretched my shoulders back and pressed my hands down even lower. It was pleasing to have her approval and, as I realised this, I felt a tingle of excitement at the base of my stomach. It spread into my crack and straight away I hoped for more of her appreciation. She did not give it, but her withholding of it sent another thrill of anticipation through my body, this time into my chest and hardening nipples.

I felt the heat of Petra's breath against my ear as she held her lips close and whispered.

'Now, Syra, I wonder if you remember which way you were facing. Probably not, even so, we need to give you a bit of a spin — just to get you started.'

Her lips touched my ear for a moment. I held my arms as rigidly as possible. She took my shoulders in her hands — she must have been standing in front of me. She turned me to the left, slowly. The first time, I knew when I was facing behind my original position and then when I had returned to face front. The second time I was not so sure. As she took me round again, I was not sure whether it was for a third time or not because I had completely lost track of what was in front of me or behind me.

She kept turning me and I started to feel dizzy. I was leaning to one side, I thought. I had to put my foot out to stop myself from falling. When I put my foot down, I wasn't sure if I was still leaning to one side or not. I fought to keep my hands by my side then, suddenly, I had to throw them out to prevent myself from falling down.

She stopped turning me. I sensed her annoyance. There was a pause. My head was buzzing and I felt I was still turning. I held my hands out at either side. I knew I was rocking unsteadily.

Suddenly I felt her grab my T shirt and pull it up angrily. I lifted my arms and she yanked the T shirt free. She did not pull it free of my head though, but instead twisted it at the top so that it wrapped tightly around my face like a hood. I gasped and reached out randomly. The heat of my breath burned my nostrils. Then I realised my breasts were bared, exposed in the meadow for anyone who was there to see. I felt my face flush hot and I panted heavily against the cotton of the T shirt that was pulled taut across my face.

'Hands by your side!'

For a moment, I hesitated. I was confused and surprised by her sudden anger.

'By your side!'

I shrieked as she pinched my nipples between her fingers and thumbs. I couldn't believe what she was doing!

'If you are given an instruction, you must follow it. That's the game, little Syra, and you must obey the rules of the game. If you don't, well I think you understand now what will happen.' She twisted my nipples sharply and I cried out again. 'Exactly, you'll be given a little reminder. Yes, Syra, that is only a little reminder'

She released my nipples. I gasped with relief. Straight away I felt a prodding finger against my bare back — I couldn't tell whether it was Petra or Robin. I stepped forward and immediately felt dizzy again. I couldn't stop myself from holding my arms out in front of me in case I fell. I knew I had done wrong, and I knew I would be punished. I snapped my arms back by my sides, but already it was too late.

'Oh, Syra, you are not doing very well with the rules. What a bad start.'

I felt hands at the buckle of my belt. Slowly, it was undone. I sensed the weight of the buckle dragging the end of the belt aside. The button at the top was undone, and then the zip was pulled down.

'Panties! Oh, Syra, you surprise me. I'm afraid that's another black mark. Oh dear, Syra. Panties!'

I kept my hands by my side — I could just about manage it — but I was swaying from side to side as my jeans were pulled down to my ankles.

'Step out, Syra. Step out.'

As I lifted my right leg, I tottered sideways and had to hold my arms out again to steady myself. She did not say anything, but I heard her heavy intake of breath and I knew I had broken the rules again.

I stood as upright as I could while my panties were pulled down. The gusset caught in the flesh of my cunt as they came down, and I tightened my buttocks and twisted my hips to relieve the tangle of material. I gasped as it pulled harder and I opened my legs enough to let it free. I felt them drop against the tops of my feet. I did not know whether to step out of them or wait to be told. I waited, but nothing was said so I stepped out of them.

I realised that now I was naked. I realised that I was standing in the middle of the meadow where everyone could see me, naked, blindfolded, and with my T short twisted up over my head in a hood. And worse, I had allowed myself to be put in this position, and I did not dare do anything unless it was an instruction from Petra or Robin. I couldn't believe how I had so quickly come under their control — how I had so easily given myself up to their mastery.

'Walk over here, Syra. Come. We cannot go further with our game until you have been made to understand the rules.'

I stepped forward. I wasn't so unsteady now but I had no idea in which direction I was walking.

'Keep coming. Yes, a few more paces.'

I did not dare reach out but, all the time, I felt worried that I would bump into something. I clenched my teeth and fought to make the effort to walk into the unknown.

'Stop!'

I stopped abruptly, worried that there was an obstacle or some other danger ahead.

'There is a picnic bench ahead. You will be approaching it from the side. Take three steps forward and then stop.'

I did as I was told. I breathed in deeply and bit onto my lips. I pressed my hands tightly against my sides. A sudden thrill ran through me. I didn't know where it came from — it was so sudden — but I knew that it was a thrill of pleasure, of anticipation, and that it was born of what was happening to me, and of what was going to happen to me.

'Stop! The seat of the bench is almost against your

shins. If you bend your knees forward they will touch the edge of it. Do it!'

The edge of the bench came against my shins — it was hard and dug into my skin.

'Now, lift you left leg and kneel on the seat.'

'I lifted my left leg and followed her instruction.

'Now the right leg. Good. Now you must bend. Reach your hands above your head and bend forward.'

I lifted my hands high above my head, still keeping my arms straight, then bent forward until I felt my nipples touching the warm slatted timber surface of the heavy bench. I stopped there — she had not said that I should lie against it, so I waited.

'Lie down against it. Allow your bottom to rise up. It needs to be fully exposed.'

I let my breasts press against the timber bench top and dropped the weight of my body against it. My bottom lifted at the same time and I tipped it up more so that my cunt could be seen between the taut join of my buttocks and thighs. I did not turn my face to the side and rested the weight of my head on my chin and the end of my nose. My cheeks were hot and flushed and, when I licked my tongue out between my lips, I tasted my warm, wet breath.

'You have done well with my last instructions, Syra, but to start with you were disobedient, and neither Robin nor I can let that pass without punishment. Let me remind you. You must follow my instructions exactly, any transgression will be punished. And any failure to take your punishment as instructed will receive further punishment and, if you continue to disobey, this process will not end. I will not ask you if you understand — I will assume you do. Now, remain still, no matter what happens, no matter how much pain you feel, you must remain still. That is your only instruction. Be still!'

I heard voices behind me — they were neither Petra nor Robin. And more to the side — women and men! I felt surrounded. I realised I had become an object of interest — something for public viewing. And I could tell by the mocking tone of their voices that I was now someone receiving public humiliation, someone to be degraded and reviled.

I felt my heart thumping in my chest. My breathing became more rapid — I was panting fast. But, I did not dare move in any way — Petra had told me to remain still.

I was there for what seemed ages — lying prone along the bench with my bottom held high, naked with the hood over my head, and only able to do as I was told.

Then I heard a swish — something moving quickly through the air. I didn't have time to think what it was. It landed across my buttocks and cut them with an intense burning pain. It felt like the slap of leather and the edges that burnt my skin felt like the edges of a belt, but I was not sure. It pulled away, its tip just catching the side of my hip as it was withdrawn. Then I heard another swish and it landed again — heavy, smacking, intense.

'That was just to let you know what to expect. Now, Syra, you will receive your proper punishment. First, for not keeping your arms by your side when instructed to do so.'

My bottom burnt as it came down again. I breathed in sharply and held it — it helped me absorb the pain. I gritted my teeth as the second one came down, and I clenched them hard with the third. There were six in total and then it stopped. I felt relieved but did not dare relax.

I waited to be told to get up. I imagined having the hood pulled from my head and the blindfold removed. I pictured myself laughing with Petra and Robin, caressing them and kissing them, before placing my head first between Petra's thighs and then Robin's. I saw myself licking their soft fleshy cunts one after another until, in the end, I took my turn and together they licked mine.

'Now, for raising your arms without being told!'

The lashing strap came down again. I was shocked from my reverie and felt sure I jolted forward. I tightened myself against it, hoping I had not moved enough to be noticed. As the next five were delivered with increasing ferocity, I bit onto my lips and held onto my screams, fixing my mind more than anything on remaining still.

'And for wearing panties!'

This time I heard my screams trying to escape. It was a pathetic whimpering but, in the end, I could not hold it back. On the sixth lashing smack I gave way and suddenly screamed out loudly.

'And that will mean more, Syra. Oh dear, you are going to feel the cutting leather of the strap much more than I thought'

I bit my lips again, but I knew it was hopeless — now I would not be able to hold my screams back.

'And for lifting your leg when not told to!'

I did not even suppress my scream on the first. It was muffled by the hood of my T shirt, but it was loud nevertheless. I just gave way to it. I lifted my bottom into the pain and the added exposure made me scream even louder. On the fourth I was screeching, but now I was also hoping that this time there would be more than six. When it stopped again I felt a wave of disappointment. The flesh of my cunt was wet and hot. Spit was running from my mouth. I sucked it back into my nostrils and swallowed it heavily. I opened my mouth wide. I knew that each scream would bring more punishment, and I wanted to scream as loudly as I possibly could.

'And for stepping out of your panties — which you shouldn't have been wearing anyway — without an instruction from me or Robin.'

And it continued, and all I heard inside the hood made by my T shirt were the screams that by now had turned into begging pleas for more.

I did not know how long it was that I did not move. In the end one of the youths who had been playing soccer pulled the wound-up T shirt from my head. Even then, I did not attempt to remove the blindfold — I still felt too controlled, too in need of instructions in order to act.

'Shall I take this blindfold off?' he asked.

I don't know whether I said anything or not, or if I nodded or gave my assent — it didn't seem important.

When it came away, I was blinded by the sudden burst of light. My head spun with it. The youth was joining his friends again by the time I could see anything. My eyes filled with tears but, slowly, things came into focus.

I saw Petra ad Robin leaning against the black Ford sedan that was parked between the other cars. A hand extended from the driver's window and held out a wad of notes. Robin took it and stuffed it into the picnic bag that hung from her shoulder. She bent forward and blew a kiss to the driver. Petra giggled and, in unison, they turned and strode away arm in arm.

The car stayed there for a few minutes. I couldn't move, I was frozen to the spot. It had to be Father Dawson! It was his car! It had to be him! But how could he be here?

How could he have found me? My mouth went dry. No, it was impossible. I was imagining things again. I was exhausted by the punishment I had received. I was bewildered by the light. I was worn out by travelling. Of course, I was confused. I must be wrong.

The window closed, the car reversed from the grassy meadow onto the road. It paused for a moment, as if giving me an opportunity for a last look, then it drove away.

My stomach filled with nerves. I started trembling. I couldn't stop myself. I was shaking all over. I thought I was going to faint. I knew it was him. It was pointless deceiving myself. He had found me. I knew it. Perhaps he had never lost me. Suddenly, I was overcome with a wave of panic. The thought that I had never truly escaped from him made my head spin. And the idea that he was pursuing me but not bothering to take me back, made me feel more insecure than ever. Seeing him like that, and watching him drive away, was worse than if he had got out and laid claim on me again. Yes, it was worse to be left there than it would be to be taken once more into his captivity. The idea that he was out there, that he knew where I was, that he could follow me at will, and that, when he chose, he could again take me under his control — it was terrifying.

When, finally, I picked up the courage to move, I ran to the pick-up and drove away as fast as I could. I should have known it was a mistake — the 20 mph speed limit is a strict rule in a state park, and I was doing 50!

The park ranger was the one who had met me at the entrance. He did not make too many demands — I would have preferred it if he had. He fucked my anus and smacked me hard across the bottom with the flat of his hand, but it was not enough — nothing like enough, and I felt deeply disappointed. I stayed on my hands and knees in the back of the pick-up and waited for him to take off his belt and give me a whipping with it, or perhaps thrash me with a stick or a rolled magazine or anything that would hurt and make me cry out for mercy. But he just spat on the floor dismissively and walked back to his truck. He looked back for a second and threw his eyes up in contempt, but even the thrill of his disdain was not enough to make me forget the new horror which had suddenly broken back into my world. I wanted something which would obliterate what I had seen. I needed something to make me forget the knowledge that, even though he had not taken possession of me yet, Father Dawson was once again my master.

12 BOSTON
THE SATYR

I drove straight to a bar and got drunk — badly drunk. All the while I imagined that Father Dawson was waiting outside, spying on me, and deciding when he would take the opportunity to reclaim me. Every few minutes I went outside to look, but there was no sinister black sedan, no one lurking in the shadows. In the end, although I was filled with anxiety, I got fed up with checking, got increasingly drunk and forgot him completely.

The next morning I woke up in an alley. I knew I had been thrashed — my bottom was red and bruised — but I couldn't remember anything about it — who had done it, how long it had lasted, or what had been used to inflict the blows. I rubbed my hand across my buttocks — they were very sore. And I was freezing cold. My blouse had been torn down the front and my left breast was exposed. My nipple was soft and pink and there were distinct red bite marks around it. I touched it and winced — it was really sensitive. I tried hard to remember what had happened, but nothing would come back.

I struggled to get up — my head was pounding, and I felt dizzy and unstable. I pulled my blouse together as well as I could. I felt dishevelled and dirty. How could I not remember what had happened to me and then wake up like this, in this state, in an alley? I felt disgusted with myself.

I saw my pick-up parked at the end of the alley. I could hardly believe it. I thought there must be someone watching over me. I winced again as I sat down on the shiny plastic bench seat. I checked in the glove compartment. I was still solvent!

I decided I needed a treat, some pampering. I booked into a Best Western just outside Boston — it had a swimming pool and spa. I thought I would rest up there before moving on. I got some strange looks when I walked into the reception — a pretty Hispanic girl behind the desk looked at me with contempt. But she took my money in advance without any argument and I dropped a five dollar bill on her desk just so that she would feel guilty about her attitude. She smiled back broadly. She had beautiful teeth.

I soaked in the bath, sat in the spa and had a massage. After two days I felt completely renewed — my fears had disappeared, my soreness had gone and I was totally refreshed. The second night, I ate with the Hispanic receptionist. She was very pretty and had a beautiful body. We slept together and the next morning, as I knelt on all fours on the edge of the swimming pool, she bound my wrists and ankles with rope and drove a cock-shaped vibrator deep into my cunt. My screams of joy echoed around the swimming pool. She said I sounded like a banshee and we both laughed and dived naked into the pool together. When the manager came in shouting and waving his arms, we climbed out, gathered our towels and ran out to the pick-up giggling and laughing. She said she didn't like working there anyway and, when I dropped her off at the 'T' subway station at Alewife, she said she was going to Florida for some sun. She kissed me passionately and ran down the platform.

I waited as she left — she looked delectable, sitting behind the glass of the subway coach. She smiled and waved enthusiastically as it pulled out — I was overcome by her youth, her vitality and her beauty.

I thought I would find some culture in Boston —

educated people everywhere — Harvard, MIT, Tufts, and all the museums.

As I wandered through the leafy streets, I began again to think of my research work, my involvement with the Greek manuscripts that I had worked on with Professor Harrington — it seemed like a lifetime ago. Suddenly, I remembered the name of someone at the Boston Museum of Art who had once helped me with some translation work— Dr Filipe Fitz. I decided to look him up to see if I could find again something of my old life — something of a life which was my own. Perhaps, I thought, I might even be able to pick up again on my work. Yes, contact with something of my past would definitely help me re-orientate myself. I had been too long on my own, trying to sort things out and getting nowhere. I felt a surge of excitement at the prospect, and I was seized by a wave of optimism at the idea of a fresh start.

The museum had only just opened for the day when I arrived. I was directed to Dr Fitz's office. It was located at the end of several grey and featureless corridors that lay behind the more appealing public façade of brightly lit and cleverly mounted exhibits in the seemingly endless galleries and halls.

I opened a door and peered around its thick steel-banded edge.

I recognised him straight away — he was tall and dark with a day's growth of beard. He sat behind a desk piled high with files and papers, a neat blue scarf wrapped loosely round his neck. A young woman in a black skirt and white blouse stood beside him taking notes. He looked up.

'I'm Syra, Syra Bond. I don't know if you remember me. I was — '

'Syra! Remember you! How could I forget you? Wow! It's so good to see you again. What a business about poor old Harrington. It was a great shock. So sudden. What am I thinking? Dulcie, get Syra a chair. Here, come and sit beside me. My, you look good. Fantastic!'

'You look pretty good yourself.'

'Syra, you're just flattering me. My, you look good! Dulcie, get us some coffee!'

Dulcie went to the coffee machine on the other side of the room.

Dr Fitz stared at me and smiled.

'Syra, I've got some important guests here today — a special exhibit, very special. I'd like to show it to you. Forget the coffee, Dulcie, but come along with us.'

He grabbed my hand and pulled me enthusiastically back out into the corridor. Dulcie followed behind.

'She's Spanish. Beautiful, don't you think?'

He was right. She was delicately formed, black haired and tanned. Her white blouse and black skirt gave her an air of competence and efficiency. She carried her notebook in her left hand and her pencil in her right. When I looked at her, she smiled quickly before demurely looking down to the ground.

'Yes, she is. What's the exhibit?'

'It's right up your street. "Slave of the Satyr King". That's what it's called. It's taken ages to mount and this is the first day it's ready to be seen. You're very honoured, Syra. Here we are.'

He led me into a dark room. Our footsteps echoed. I couldn't see anything. The door closed behind us with a dull thud. Dulcie switched on the lights.

'What do you think, Syra? Is that magnificent or what? Our latest exhibit — "Slave of the Satyr King". Ancient

Greece has come to Boston in a big way don't you think?'

It was a huge room. On three sides were statues of the Bacchii — drunken revellers — spilling goblets clutched in their hands, their arms around in other in inebriated bonhomie as they luxuriated in the pleasures of debauched drunkenness. The third side was bare black glass. In the centre, and the attention of the drunken Bacchanalians, a satyr — half man, half beast — his pipes to his mouth, his massive erect phallus pressing upwards from his fur-covered legs.

'Isn't he just magnificent, Syra. Look at his phallus! Have you ever seen such an erection! It's often asked what it must have been like to have a satyr's cock. What do you think, Syra? Can you imagine it?'

Dr Fitz walked over to the satyr. Dulcie followed behind. Her face was flushed and she looked down at her feet.

'Dulcie finds it embarrassing, don't you Dulcie?'

Dulcie shuffled her feet. For an instant I saw a flash of her white panties reflected in the glossy black of her shiny leather shoes. I could hardly believe it, but when I looked again she had moved her feet and the delightful image had gone. I smiled at her, but she was too embarrassed to look up at me.

'No matter. Syra, what do you think?'

I walked over to join him. The satyr was so lifelike — I could hardly believe it was a statue.

'He looks so real. Can I touch him?'

'Of course. Touch any apart of him you want!' He bent and whispered in my ear. 'In any way you want, Syra, any way at all.'

The satyr had a large nose, leathery skin and two half curled horns protruding from his large head. I reached out to touch his shoulders but, just as I made contact, I drew back sharply

'What's the matter, Syra? He won't bite!'

'I could have sworn I saw his eyes move! Really! He suddenly turned his eyes and looked at me!'

Dr Fitz laughed.

'Syra! You always did have an active imagination. Now, I've got to go and greet my guests. Is it okay if I leave you alone for a while? The satyr will keep his eye on you, I'm sure!'

He laughed again and went out through the heavy door, Dulcie following behind with her notebook and pencil at the ready. As the door closed, she looked back at me. She frowned and tightened her lips in a look of concern. I heard Dr Fitz call her from the corridor and she disappeared.

I walked around the figures of the Bacchii. Like the satyr, they were unbelievably real. Their skin look so warm and lifelike and, when I plucked up enough courage to touch one on the arm, it felt exactly like a living person. It was amazing. I went back and walked around the satyr. His bent goat-like legs and hoofed feet were incongruous against his fine muscular torso and heavily muscled arms. He had a broad forehead and wrinkled skin, and his large, hooked nose and curling horns brought together a mixture of beast and man that took my breath away. I had studied vases with images of satyrs, but I had never been in the presence of one before! And that was exactly how it felt. As if I was in the presence of a living satyr.

I smiled at my own fantasy. I stood alongside him and posed, as if I was having my picture taken. Cautiously, I draped my arm across his shoulder and put on a wide cheesy grin. I pulled away and laughed at myself — it was all very stupid. I went along the line of Bacchii. I touched some of them, again cautiously at first but, as I became more used to it, in a normal and relaxed fashion. I imagined myself drinking with them, sharing their jokes, enjoying their attention, their drunken leering, and their corny wisecracks. I stopped by one and peered into his face — frozen in the act of breaking into laughter. I looked at his goblet, brimful and ready to spill down his rich gold and purple robes. I saw something odd, a shimmering reflection. It was coming from the surface of the drink in the goblet. I pressed my finger down onto it. It was liquid, the goblet was full of liquid!

I drew back in surprise. I hadn't expected the drinks to be real. It was amazing! The attention to detail was fantastic! I walked again along the line of Bacchii — their drunken faces frozen; some caught in a smile, some a leer, and some trying to hold back a noisy outburst of temper. I reached forward and touched one on the chin. I pulled my hand back quickly; afraid he might suddenly come to life. I smiled at my silliness and went and stood next to the satyr — balanced precariously on his hooves, his thick furred legs bent at the knee, his thighs wide and muscular. His two hands were either side of his pipes as all his fingers were frozen, poised over the holes.

Suddenly, I heard a noise behind me! I turned — startled and shaking. I looked at the goblet of one of the Bacchii — drink was spilling over its side! There was no one to be seen anywhere!

I turned back to the satyr. One of his hands was now by his side! And he seemed to be looking at me. I held my breath. I was terrified. An ice-cold shiver ran up my back. I bit my lips. This was ridiculous! Impossible! Suddenly, there was another sound behind me.

I heard a goblet dropping to the ground, and wine sloshing from it. I thought I heard the sound of someone stumbling to pick it up but, when I turned, nothing was moving. Confused and filled with anxiety, I looked again at the satyr — now, he was holding his pipes loosely at his side!

I felt beads of cold sweat on my forehead. I backed away from him. I couldn't believe what I was seeing. My legs felt shaky. I slipped on the wine that had spilled on the floor and fell clumsily onto my back. I looked around bewildered, struggling hopelessly to get back to my feet. Suddenly, the room was full of noise — shouting, laughter, and voices raised in anger. I sensed movement all around me. I was trembling all over. I closed my eyes tightly and clapped my hands over my ears. I didn't know what was going on.

Someone came up behind me and grabbed my shoulders. Strong hands twisted me onto my knees. Someone else tipped some wine over my head. I tasted it as it ran down my cheeks and onto my chin — strong, acidic, full bodied and heavy. Another goblet of wine was sloshed over my head. It ran in my hair and down my face. I sucked it up my nostrils as I struggled for breath. It burned the back of my throat. I choked and coughed. There was laughter all around me.

I felt a sharp jabbing in my sides. Some of the Bacchii were prodding me with sticks, driving me forward on my hands and knees, taunting me, laughing at me if I did not go the right way or could not go fast enough. I yelped as they drove the sticks in. One of them slashed his stick across my bottom. I turned as I cried out. He looked down menacingly and brought it down again viciously.

He shouted at me. It was Ancient Greek — Attic

perhaps — but I could not make out the strange dialect. He shouted again. I looked at him blankly. He raised his cane and whipped it down on my bottom. I lifted my hands off the ground and sat upright on my knees. It made him angrier, he pushed me in the back and I dropped down again onto all fours.

He shouted again at the top of his voice. It was gibberish to me. Two of them grabbed my hips and pulled at the waistband of my jeans. They struggled with the button and grabbed at the zip without any idea of how it worked. They shouted as well — frustrated and angry with their failed attempts to strip me bare.

The first one roared again. The others fumbled more but still they could not get the button undone. I felt their increasing irritation as they twisted and snatched at the denim material. It pulled against my hips and dug into me. The tight crotch snatched at the flesh of my cunt. The cane came down again repeatedly. I lifted my hands off the ground and tried to sit up. I was forced back again and one of them pinned my hands down beneath his feet.

I looked up as one of them approached with a large curved knife in his hand. He held it threateningly against my cheek. It was cold and smooth. I felt the sharp glistening edge digging into my skin. I didn't know what was going to happen. I shivered with uncontrollable fear.

He shouted out loudly, dropped to his knees and drove the blade between the bare skin of my hips and the material of my jeans which covered them. He pulled it downwards and, in one slashing cut, he rent the material from the waist half way down to the knee.

They all clamoured around to look. He jumped up, went to the other side and did the same. I felt the cold edge of the steel blade against my thigh as it severed the denim as though it was paper. The one with the cane pulled the torn material down and uncovered my naked bottom — I had no panties on. A roar went up. He waited for a moment as they all stared at my buttocks, then he brought the cane down again as hard as he could.

I screamed out — the pain shot through my body in a sudden jolting shock. I threw my head back and gasped for breath. I knew it would come again and I tensed myself, but as the cane landed on my naked skin, the shock was even greater than before. It was so sharp, so penetrating, and I was defenceless against its stabbing attack. I was overtaken by it — it consumed me.

My hands were released and I was driven around the room with the cane. They all laughed at my predicament and, when I yelled out as another cutting blow came down on my bottom, they shouted out their approval and demands for more.

I scuttled on my hands and knees — my heart pounding, my mouth gaping with fear and panic. Spit dribbled from my mouth as blow after cutting blow from the cane came down across my red striped buttocks. My body jolted in pain with every stroke that the cane delivered, and my innards burned as they were licked with the harsh fire it lit in me.

They drove me into a corner and ripped the slashed jeans down over my feet. They pulled at my T shirt and dragged it roughly over my head. I hung my head in shame as they emptied their wine goblets over me. It poured in streams across my back and bottom, down between my thighs and into ruby red pools around my knees. It ran through my hair, into my ears and down my cheeks. It ran into the corners of my mouth and streamed off my chin. I felt wretched and humiliated. Their laughter only added to my indignity as, on my hands and knees, dripping with wine and facing a corner of the room, I was overcome with a deep sense of shame and disgrace.

Their jabbering became hushed. Wine continued to run over my back and buttocks, but the drunken Bacchii were no longer pouring any more over me. I heard a strange clattering sound — a harsh stamping — I could not make out what it was. A shadow fell across me. I looked down between my open legs and saw two brown hooves and two fur covered legs — it was the satyr!

I felt my already thumping heart quicken even more. I thought it was going to explode. I bit on my lips but I was shaking so much I could not keep them together and spit oozed between them in a frothy stream. My fear had overcome me — I crouched on my hands and knees shivering and feeling completely out of control.

The Bacchii began chanting — a slow measured drone. In the corner of my eye, I saw them rocking from side to side. I heard the hooves again — they moved closer between my knees. I felt the harsh fur of the satyr's legs against the insides of my thighs. The droning dirge rose and fell. I felt the heat of the satyr's huge erect phallus against the naked skin of my buttocks. Its tip radiated heat — intense and searing. He brought it closer and it touched the skin in the valley between the taut cheeks of my upturned bottom. Its searing heat was tremendous.

The Bacchii's chorus dropped to a hum. The satyr moved the heavy throbbing end of his massive cock between the split of my buttocks. I felt its burning tip against the ring of my anus. I dropped my mouth open as I realised he was pushing it in.

My eyes widened as it entered — I could not believe it would go in. The Bacchii's song increased in volume.

The satyr's cock slid in — bit by pounding bit it entered the tight confines of my rectum. I could not bring my lips together and spit ran from my trembling mouth in a bubbling stream. I dropped my head low to the ground as I was speared by his gigantic cock. I was pushed forward until the back of my neck was forced against the corner of the room. It kept penetrating me, never stopping or easing back, until suddenly, when I could not imagine how I could possibly take more, I felt it expanding as a flooding stream of semen ran along its venous length.

He clung to my hips with his talon-like fingers then tightened them against my skin as he drove it in one last time. I felt his rough furred thighs tightly pressed against my buttocks and, as I held my breath and stared wide-eyed between my legs, I felt myself filled with his great stream of bubbling, scalding semen. It ran inside me and saturated me. I coughed and choked. It was as if my throat was full of it. I slumped in his grip as he continued to drain himself inside me, and I felt my eyes closing with half-conscious exhaustion as finally he drew it out.

As I heard his semen bubbling around my anus, I felt myself pushing back against it. Instead of being relieved by its withdrawal, I felt myself wanting to get closer to it, wanting to receive more of its hot elixir. I opened my buttocks wide, showing him where he had been, and I cried out in a joyful scream of ecstasy and fulfilment as he drove his mighty cock back in.

It slid in on his semen and I rode its full length, thrusting myself back onto it, squirming around it, pushing as hard as I could to get every pulsating part of it as deeply inside as possible. My ecstasy overcame me — I did not know what was happening. The Bacchii gathered round, still chanting and, as if carrying out some pagan sacrament, in unison they emptied their wine goblets over me. I was soaked. I felt I could drown in it and, as I looked back between my legs I saw a continuous stream of semen running from my dilated and still-filled anus.

Suddenly, the blank wall was illuminated. A crowd of people were on the other side, sitting in rows on three tiers of chairs. Some of them were pointing, some laughing, one of the women in the front row — her satin dress off her shoulders — was pouting her red lipstick-coated lips and attending to her fingernails. A man at the back had his cock in his hand and was squeezing it as his semen ran into the mouth of a woman on her knees in front of him. It was Dulcie! Her head was back, her mouth wide open. Her luxurious full lips were wet from her spit and, as she gaped upwards, they were splattered with the man's copious semen. She pulled at the front of her white blouse and exposed her small, pert breasts. Her pink nipples were hard and prominent. She let his semen run over her tongue. Only when he had completely drained it did she close her mouth and swallow. She licked her lips and looked up at him, as if asking him if there was any more. He turned away and she reached over and picked up her notebook and pencil which were on the floor by her knees.

As I stared at her, the heavy door behind me opened.

Dr Fitz walked in keenly ahead of a group of men.

'There gentlemen, isn't that the most amazing exhibit you've ever seen. What a show! And look at our poor slave. See how she remains on her hands and knees — shamed and humiliated, and yet still waiting for her master to use her again when he chooses.'

For a moment I could not move, then, as if caught up in an irresistible tide, I felt overwhelmed by a great surge of pleasure inside me. I crawled forward as it ran from my cunt up inside my rectum. I could not hold it in, nor resist it. I crawled forward between the silent still figures and stopped at Dr Fitz's feet. I looked up at him and he started to undo the zip to his trousers.

The next morning, as I walked away from the museum, I realised how I had deceived myself. I could not get my old life back — it was impossible. I had gone too far away from it ever to return. The only way for me was forward. There was no alternative — I was locked irredeemably onto only that path. But where did the path lead? Ahead, all I could see was more suffering, more humiliation, and more degradation. The thought of it filled me with fear but, as the shiver of dread passed through me, it was accompanied by an exciting tremor of anticipation. Yes, I could only go forward.

13. CONCORD
USED

I spent the morning in Concord — I wanted to visit the home of Emerson, Thoreau and Louisa May Alcott. It had rained hard — soaking eastern seaboard rain. I was wearing only a T shirt and shorts and I was soaked. I walked down Main Street looking for some shelter. I pushed my way between self-infatuated Ivy League fathers earnestly training their even more self-infatuated candidate sons in the arts of assertion, mathematics, social superiority, and ignorance for their fellow man. The whole place was twee and self-engrossed — antique shops, bookstores, prissy cafés and pretention. I couldn't imagine Thoreau feeling comfortable here at all — perhaps that's why he went to live in the woods.

Just before the junction with Walden Street the road tightened up to a pedestrian crossing. An attractive, pale skinned woman stood in the doorway of a sports shop — "Marcia's Sports". She held a bright pink umbrella over her head — she was wet and shivering.

'They have some great prices here, sweetie. Get something warm for a few dollars. It looks as though you need it.'

I smiled at her. I felt sorry for her. One of the strainers in her umbrella had broken through the cover and rain was dripping down the front of her shirt. I could see she wasn't wearing a bra.

'Are you going to come in?' I asked her. 'You look cold too.'

'Not just yet. You go in though. You won't regret it.'

She shivered, took out a tissue from a small pocket in her short pleated skirt and blew her nose.

I went in as she held the door open. It was a big store, filled with clothing and sports equipment. A young girl asked me what I needed.

'Something dry, and cheap.'

She grabbed some clothing off a rail and escorted me to a changing room. It was huge — white painted walls, shiny marble tiles, a soft sofa and a pine, slatted bench.

'Help yourself and take your time. There's no rush. Enjoy.'

I pulled my T shirt over my head. A mist of water sprayed from my hair. My nipples were hard and wet. I shivered. My jeans were sodden and, when I dropped them on the floor, water ran from them to form a pool.

As I stood naked and dripping wet with my soaked panties in my hands — the louvered barroom style doors swung open.

A haughty looking man stood behind a white-faced youth. After what I had seen in the town, I imagined it must be a father and his son.

'Go on,' urged the man. 'There's nothing to be afraid of.'

The youth moved forward nervously.

'Will you be long, miss?' he enquired. The man prodded him in the back. 'I ... I have an item I wish to try on.'

He held forward an oversized football shirt with "Harvard" emblazoned across the chest.

'No need to justify yourself, Henry.'

'Sorry ... sorry, sir.'

'No need to apologise either, Henry.'

'No, sir ... sorry, sir.'

I smiled.

'I don't mind sharing,' I said. 'Feel free. There's plenty of room in here.'

The man looked at the youth and nodded. The youth looked around nervously. The man scowled at him and prodded him again.

The man could not take his eyes from my body. His fixed stare followed down from my breasts, across my stomach to the slit of my cunt — naked and glistening from the wetness of my soaked panties and already responding to the situation I had found myself in.

Again he jabbed the boy in the back.

'Go on, my boy. Go on.'

The boy stepped forward again. I felt the heat of his body. I felt his fear.

Still staring at my cunt, the man extended his hand onto the boy's shoulder. But the boy had become fixed to the spot — he was completely unable to move.

'Henry, I think perhaps you should wait it out for a while. Go and choose another item. Think things over. Remember what I told you. Be positive. Come back when you feel more comfortable.'

The youth turned and went. He didn't need a second prompting.

'You're staying?' I asked.

'If you don't mind?'

'Not at all. You can help me if you like.'

He looked behind him and stepped in beside me. He stroked his hand along the side of my hip and reached between the tops of my thighs. It felt good. I rose up onto his fingers then dropped myself against their tips. They slipped in on the moisture that covered my flesh — already hot and swollen with excitement and urgency. I sighed as they went in deeply — it was delightful.

He massaged the soft flesh of my cunt and pressed his thumb and forefinger around the swelling bud of my clitoris. My already hard nipples ached. He dropped his mouth around them in turn, sucking and biting each one with a fevered passion. The ache in them turned to pain and that, as it circled them and ran up into my throat in rolling waves, turned to a different sort of ache — an ache for more.

Suddenly, he pulled back and yanked the leather belt from his trousers. It came free with a sharp snap.

'On your knees!' he said brusquely.

I was surprised by his sudden change of tone, but I did not question his instruction for a moment — it was forthright, so commanding. I felt as if I had no option. I dropped to my knees and felt a surge of delight at my immediate and unquestioning obedience to his order. I looked up into his eyes, waiting for another instruction.

'Put your hands together, as if you're praying, then hold them up.'

The aching in my nipples increased. I felt the moisture of my cunt. I squirmed my legs together. I did what he said.

He wrapped the belt around my wrists, pulled the strap through the buckle and yanked it up as much as it would go. I cried out as the hard edge of the leather belt dug into the skin of my wrists. He looked at me angrily.

'Look, it's more than my life's worth not to do this. Do you get me? I've no option. Don't think I want to do this to you. No, don't think that, but I have to. I just have to.'

He was obviously worried. It was as if he was scared of something, or someone.

'Look, just do as I say and it'll be alright. Really it will. It'll be trouble for me if you don't though.'

He pulled my bound wrists up to a coat hook on the wall. He latched the strap over the hook.

'Stay on your knees. I need you stretched up.'

He went back to the swing doors and anxiously looked out into the shop.

'And I'll put this across your mouth. It's better if I do. It's a football chinstrap. Open your mouth.'

I opened my mouth. I felt a fresh surge of heat in the flesh of my cunt as I obeyed him.

'Wider! That's better. Press your tongue against the back of it. It'll stop you gagging.'

He pulled the plastic chinstrap into my mouth. I pushed my tongue against it — it tasted sweet and sickly. It had four elastic straps, two on each side, and, as he pulled them back, they dug into the corners of my mouth. They had notched loops at the ends to fit to a football helmet. He pulled these firmly around my head and wound them together at the back. They were extremely tight.

'Good.'

I hung on the straps at my wrists, my mouth tightly gagged by the chinstrap, naked and with droplets of rain still glistening on my cold wet skin. I could not believe what had happened — it had been so fast. It seemed incredible that within a few minutes I had found my way into this situation. Five minutes ago I was walking outside in the road, soaking wet, and now I was bound and gagged, hanging on a hook on the wall of a changing room and obeying every instruction of a man I had never seen before — and a man whose name I didn't even know.

'Look, it's like this,' he said hurriedly. 'I have to do it. When I first met her, Marcia that is, it was love at first sight. I was bewitched. It was incredible, but it wasn't long before things changed. She was never satisfied She always wanted more than I could give — more money, more clothes, more sex. I tried my best. I really did. I took an extra job in a club and did without a lot of things I would have liked, but she was insatiable. Soon, she started bringing young men home. It was always young men, and always inexperienced. That was what she liked, young men who knew nothing of sex. She liked to "train them up" as she put it. Well, she certainly trained them up — and me along with them. I soon found myself looking after her as though I was her servant. Every day I would clean the house and prepare it for the evenings when she brought her young men home. And she insisted I always watched. Yes, I used to sit on the sofa as she trained her young men. She trained them in everything and I watched it all. Do you find it exciting? The idea of me watching like that?'

I nodded.

'I can tell you exactly what she did if you want?'

I nodded again, this time more than once. The story was exciting me more than I could imagine — I could feel it deep in my cunt. I nodded again.

'Well, the first time it was a sophomore college student. I don't know where she found him. Later she put adverts in magazines and the local paper. To start with, though, she just went to student bars and picked them up. He was keen, this first one — mighty keen. She told me to sit on the sofa and watch. She said I could take my trousers down if I wanted. "Jerk off if you need to", she said. She stood the student in the centre of the room, knelt at his feet and undid his trousers. I can tell you, my cock was as hard as rock in a second!'

Suddenly, the swing doors of the changing room opened. A young man with long dark hair and a ring in his ear stood uncertainly at the entrance. When he saw me, he flushed with embarrassment and went to turn back.

'Sorry. Sorry. I must be — '

The man grabbed his arm.

'It's okay. You're in the right place. Have you got your receipt?'

The young man offered a small piece of white paper. The man took it from him, looked at it, and pushed it into his pocket.

'I see you've brought something with you. Excellent. A table tennis bat. That's a good choice.' He looked at me. 'Now, you. Stand up!'

I struggled to get up and he walked impatiently towards me. He lifted his hand to strike me across the face. He laughed as I stood up trembling and he unhooked my wrists from the hook.

'Bend over that bench!' He looked at the young man. 'Is that suitable?'

The young man nodded.

I knelt down at the end of the bench and bent forward. I knew what was going to happen — it was obvious. I was caught with two desires: whether I wanted only to follow the man's instructions, or whether I wanted to feel the bat across my bottom. As the question flittered through my mind, I realised I wanted both. And I submitted to both.

I stretched my bound wrists forward and lay prone along the slatted wooden bench. The cool hard wood pressed against my nipples. I dropped my full weight down and lifted my buttocks.

'I see you have paid for six,' he said to the young man. 'Good. Begin when you want. But, remember, only six.'

I tensed myself as I waited. The young man shuffled his feet. Then I heard the swishing sound as the bat was brought down. It smacked loudly across both cheeks of my buttocks. I pushed my tongue forward against the chinstrap in my mouth. I wanted to cry out but, even as I felt it erupting from my throat, it was stifled in a heavy bubbling burst of breath.

My heart was pounding as I heard the swish of the next. It smacked again — loud, sudden and painful. My buttocks stung. I pressed my tongue hard against the chinstrap and sucked air in through my flaring nostrils.

There was a pause, then the swishing sound again, and, in the next moment, the flat dimpled surface of the bat struck me again. My body lurched forward against the slatted bench, but there was nowhere for it to go and it simply pressed harder against the unforgiving surface. I had sharp pains in my nipples and, as spit filled my mouth, I gulped as well as I could with my tongue pressed against the back of the chinstrap.

I tightened my buttocks together and, as I did, I felt the pressure of the tops of my thighs against the soft flesh of my cunt. I could feel its wetness and warmth. I squeezed at tight as I could.

The bat came down again.

'Four!' shouted the man.

The stinging set me on fire. I breathed in heavily through my nostrils and pressed my tongue as hard as I could against the back of the plastic chinstrap.

'Five!'

I lifted my bottom to meet it. The sting was more than I could stand and yet I rose towards it, squeezed my buttocks together to absorb it and, as I realised that there was only one to go, I felt a pang of desperate regret that there would be no more.

I pressed my nose between two of the wooden slats of the bench. My nostrils were tight against their edges. I listened to my heavy laboured breathing. Spit started to bubble from the corners of my mouth. I lifted my bottom.

'Six!'

The smacking sound filled my ears. A heavy surge of heat exploded from my cunt and blasted through my whole body. Every nerve was on fire. My head spun. I heard myself blubbering spit from the edges of the chinstrap. As the sound of the smacking bat slowly dissipated, I felt the heat of my own joy filling me with ecstasy. It overcame me and I was lost to it.

I stayed lying across the bench after he had gone. Every few seconds I jerked with a fresh shuddering wrench that, although the product of my own pleasure, was stirred from the pain inflicted by the smacking bat. I knew how reddened my bottom was, and I knew how sore it felt. I longed to reach around with my hand and rub it, but the tight binding of my wrists, and my inability to move unless instructed, only sent fresh jolts of joy through my trembling body. I licked the back of the chinstrap and felt spit running onto my chin.

I waited. The man carried on with his story as though nothing had happened. I felt another wave of pleasure run through me as I revelled in his ignorance of my pain and humiliation.

'Now, where was I? Oh, yes, the first time Marcia brought a young man to the house. Well, you know, as soon as she started to suck him I just took out my cock and jerked off there and then. I let my semen run down my hand. It was great and, after she had sucked the young man's cock, and taken all his semen into her mouth, she came and licked mine and swallowed that too. Some of it stuck to her face and she rubbed it off with the back of her hand then licked that as well.

'After that, we did it all the time. She would pick up a young man, bring him back and I would watch. She always took a small fee, nothing too much, more to cover expenses really, but they were always glad to pay for their "instruction".

'Most of all, I liked watching them spank her. Don't get me wrong. I enjoyed seeing her fucked, or watching her suck cocks, but seeing her bottom raised up, round and taut, and watching it redden as she took her punishment — that took some beating. To start with they would use the flat of their hand but soon she introduced them to other methods. She would bend over a chair and they would smack her with a flat bat or a wooden paddle. She bought different things for them to use, she kept a real nice selection — riding crops, short and long tailed whips, canes of all varieties. She said the riding crops were the most painful but she never asked them to hold back. She said it was her mission in life, to "educate" young men in the ways of sex, and she must be prepared to sacrifice herself.'

Suddenly, the louvered doors swung open again. Another young man stood there anxiously holding a receipt in his hand.

'Come in, my boy, everything is ready for you.'

The man looked at the young man's ticket.

'Good choice. Very good choice.'

The young man walked over to me, wrapped his arm beneath my hips and lifted my buttocks up high. He put his foot on the bench and dropped me across his knee. I hung draped across it, unable to support myself in any way. My face lay sideways against the slatted bench.

The first one came suddenly — hard, jolting and loud. I didn't have time to breathe in again before the next came down. I drew breath in through my nostrils just as the next landed. My bottom burned and the next came down and set it on fire. And the next made me press my tongue hard against the chinstrap, and the next made me tighten my whole body as if I was having a seizure, and when the next came I realised that this time there would be more than six.

I don't know how many times he spanked me, but it was hard and fast and, when finally he did stop, I realised my body was jerking in time with my punishment. I carried on twitching like this for ages after he had gone. It subsided only slowly and, as it passed, and I gradually regained my senses, I realised that I had been hung back on the coat hook and the man was again recalling the story of his experiences with Marcia.

I don't know how long I hung on the strap around my wrists — it felt like hours. I had my eyes closed when the louvered swing doors opened again. My eyes were wide in an instant. I expected to see another young man but, this time, it was a woman —the young woman with the umbrella who had greeted me outside the shop. She stood just inside the changing room as the doors swung to behind her.

'Marcia! About time! On your knees!' shouted the man. 'You've kept me waiting long enough. But you can answer for that later — I have something in mind already. Take those wet clothes off! And get on your knees!'

This was Marcia! How could this be Marcia?

The man undid the straps at my wrists. My arms dropped suddenly as the binding came undone. My shoulders ached. I rubbed my hands. My wrists had red circles around them. He did not even undo the elastic straps of the chinstrap; he just pulled it up roughly over my head. It tugged painfully at the corners of my mouth. I coughed the chinstrap out.

I stretched my mouth, it was stiff and sore. I looked up at the man. I had to speak.

'I don't understand. How can this be Marcia? I thought she was your mistress. I thought you did as she instructed. That's what you told me.'

The man threw his head back and laughed.

'So easily duped. You're a joke. What was your name? It doesn't matter. Go on. I'm finished with you now. Marcia needed a break, but she's back now. Go on, clear off! What an idiot!'

He flopped down on the sofa and undid his trousers. He took out his burgeoning cock and held its stiff shaft in his hand.

'Come on Marcia, do your stuff. I have a living to make.'

For a moment, I was confused, then I realised. Of course, it had all been a trick. How could I have imagined that the man was Marcia's slave? Of course he wasn't — he was the master and she was his slave. It was obvious now, and he had used me to fill in while Marcia was taking a break. How could I have been so foolish! My face flushed red — I was so embarrassed, so shamed. I just wanted to run away and hide.

I pulled on my wet T shirt and jeans. They were freezing cold. I shivered all over. I pushed the swing doors open as another young man was walking towards them clutching a till receipt. Marcia was already on her knees, naked, bound by the wrists and hanging hopelessly from the coat hook on the changing room wall. I bit my lips and ran out of the shop into the pouring rain.

14. Sleepy Hollow
THE PAIN OF ATHALA, CAPE COD

I stayed for a night at the Colonial Inn. It was my special treat, but I did not enjoy it — everything was too quaint, too much of a set-up, too fictitious. I sat on the edge of the bath and masturbated before breakfast. As I finished, I bent my head down between my knees and licked the side of the bath — it tasted of bath oil.

My heart was still thumping when I went down to breakfast. As I ate my toast, I smelled the silky wetness of my cunt on my fingers, and I couldn't stop myself pushing them back down the front of my jeans. One of the waiters saw me and smirked. I licked my tongue out at him and carried on. I finished again, still with toast and marmalade in my mouth, and I licked my tongue out again as the waiter brought his supervisor and pointed at me.

I booked out and walked down to Monument Square. I stared up at the needle-like commemoration of the 'Concord Fight', the battle which had taken place about half a mile away at North Bridge in 1775. It had been the beginning of the armed conflict against Great Britain which, eventually, had led to American Independence. It made me think of the conflict which was inside me — the never-ending struggle between pain and satisfaction — and wondered if that would ever be resolved.

I strolled out of the town on Monument Street to Sleepy Hollow Cemetery — resting place of, amongst ten thousand others, Ralph Waldo Emerson, Henry David Thoreau, and Louisa May Alcott.

Five athletic girls wearing silky shorts and singlets ran past me in a group. Their breasts — firmly enclosed in tight sports bras — hardly declared themselves beneath their tops. Each had a mass of long hair tied in a ponytail — standard style for female cross-country runners in the US. Their heavy swatches of hair tossed from side to side as they ran— three striking the same rhythm, the other two adding an exciting, random syncopation to the regular pattern of their urgent movements. The leading girl, a delicately featured Oriental, smiled as they came to a halt. She pressed a button on her watch, nodded to the others and they began to run again.

I noticed how the material of her shorts pulled tightly into the crack of her cunt. I smiled back. She knew I had noticed. She was, above the others, supremely delectable. Her delicate features, pale skin and perfect proportions blended together into a representation of beauty beyond compare. I just stared at her as she ran on — her mouth closed, her cheeks revealing only the slightest blush, her thick, black, heavy mass of hair wafting from side in time with her muscular yet easy strides.

I swallowed hard and felt my heart beating fast at the thought of her. I imagined peeling off her singlet, undoing her bra at the back, then kneeling before her and slowly pulling down her shorts. They would stick to her cunt, not much, but enough to tug at the delicate flesh. And when her shorts fell around her ankles, I would stare at the cleft of her slit before slowly reaching forward and sliding my tongue along the front of the precise crack of her fragrant, faultless cunt.

She turned around to look as they rounded the wall which enclosed the cemetery. Again, she pressed a button on her watch as though she was setting herself a target or recording something she needed to remember. I blinked and they were gone.

I went in through the iron gate and climbed up the wooded rise to Authors' Ridge. I stared down at Thoreau's simple gravestone. A sudden wind rustled the leaves of the trees around me. I felt a chill of cold and shivered.

'You look cold,' I heard someone say.

I turned. A young woman stood behind me. She was tall and dressed in black and purple. She had back triangles painted around her eyes, her hair was shaved at the sides of her head and, on top, a spiked up band of light green hair in Mohican style ran down its centre. Her lips were heavily painted with black lipstick. She wore a tightly laced leather corset, a diaphanous short black skirt, black fishnet tights with holes at the knees, and long black gloves that finished just above her elbows.

'Yes, I am cold,' I said, taken aback by her sudden and dramatic appearance. 'I didn't see you when I walked up here.'

'I rose up from the ground. Here, come with me. You need something to keep you warm. Where are you from? England, I bet. My name's Sublime. Marcia told me about you. She said she thought you might be looking for something we could offer. Our patrol saw you earlier.'

She walked ahead and I followed. She took long strides and I found it hard to keep up.

'Keep up,' she called back without turning. 'You don't want to get lost here. They'll never find you again. That's if someone is looking for you in the first place.'

I jogged a few steps to catch her up.

'What do you mean, "if someone is looking for me"?'

'Nothing, sweetie. Don't get uptight.'

Her words reminded me of Father Dawson, and I felt a sudden wave of panic. I ran again to stop her getting too far in front.

'Here! Down here!'

She opened a heavy iron-spiked gate and led me into a small area surrounded on three sides by drooping heavy, black chains. On the remaining side, built into the slope of the hill was a stone built entrance to a tomb. I had seen it before, or at least something that looked just like it — a couple of years back, in Camden, New Jersey with Professor Harrington. And it carried the same inscription over the entrance "burial vault — on a sloping wooded hill — grey granite — un-ornamental — surroundings: trees, turf, sky, a hill everything crude and natural".

'We should find a bit of heat for your here, I think.'

She bent and entered beneath the massive pitched granite lintels.

'Come on! It's dark inside!'

I looked back to see if anyone was about then ducked my head and went inside.

I couldn't see anything! It was pitch-dark!

I held my hands out in front of me, turning slowly from side to side. Something stuck to my hands — something clammy! I pulled back and shook my hands to get rid of it. Whatever it was it wound itself around my wrists! I shook my hands in panic. I felt the pounding of my heart in my throat.

'There's something on my hands! Something around my wrists!'

I heard laughter. Suddenly there was light — blinding light. A flaring torch had been lit. I turned my face away. I looked at my hands. They were covered in cobwebs.

Slowly, my eyes got used to the brightness and I calmed down. Sublime was standing in front of me holding a burning torch in her hand.

'Come on. They're waiting. Quickly!'

I followed her down a passageway. Sparks crackled from the flaming torch and landed on the ground around Sublime's booted feet. It was as if she was walking on fire.

The tunnel opened up into a large cavern. Dark figures lined the walls. Sublime stopped and placed the torch in an iron stand.

'I have brought her, master, as you instructed,' she announced.

She stood aside and indicated me with her outstretched hand. A figure stepped forward. His voice boomed out.

'I am Athala. You are a lost soul seeking salvation?'

He came into the light of the torch. He was tall and dark. His straight black hair hung down over his shoulders, his purple robe trailed to the ground, his face was pale, and his eyes dark.

'Speak! Are you seeking salvation?'

My blood ran cold!

'Speak!' he shouted.

I trembled as I spoke — his words were so powerful, so commanding, I could say nothing else.

'Yes.'

'Sublime! Undress her. She needs to be naked.'

Sublime slowly undid the buttons of the blouse I had eventually bought to replace my wet T shirt. I shivered with a burst of excitement as my breasts were revealed. I looked down and saw my nipples hardening. She drew the blouse over my shoulders. It was cold inside the huge cavern and I shivered again as goose-pimples came up on my breasts. She undid my jeans and slipped them down to my ankles. I was wearing light blue panties and I squirmed my hips as she tugged them down. They caught in the flesh of my cunt — I felt the delightful tug as the flesh was pulled by the clinging material. She rested them just above my knees as one by one, she lifted my feet off the ground and removed the jeans then, after looking at my cunt for a moment, she drew the panties off over my feet in the same way.

I stood naked, my arms by my side, my nipples aching with hardness, my cunt hot and wet with the moisture of excitement and anticipation.

'Now, you may approach,' said Athala. 'But not standing. You are not fit as yet to stand in the presence of Athala. You must kneel first, show me your need for penitence, and then I may allow you to crawl before me.'

I kept my knees together and knelt. I sat up straight and felt the tension between my shoulders and down my back. I wondered if he wanted me to put my hands together — to show him how much I needed his forgiveness. I could only think of being a penitent — laying my sins before him, letting him decide if he would offer to show me some light in my dark and hopeless life. I lifted my hands and pressed my palms together then put the tips of my fingers against my trembling lips. I felt my lips moving in a silent prayer — a prayer to Athala and the forgiveness which he held in his hands.

'I see your desperation, my child. Sublime! You have done well to find her. Here! A reward for a faithful pet.'

Sublime went to him and dropped to her knees at his feet. She looked up into his dark eyes. He opened his robe and revealed his throbbing cock, standing rigidly at an upward angle from the base of his flat stomach.

'You may suck it for a few moments. I will allow you to take it deep into your throat, but not to hold it with your hands. Perhaps another time, when you have served me again, I will allow that.'

I watched as Sublime slowly pressed her black lips against the pulsating tip of his cock. Her mouth opened as she contacted the hot burgeoning surface. It slid in — she did not pause. I watched first the tip enter then, as her throat tightened and her cheeks dished in, I watched the heavy, beating shaft enter until its base pressed hard against her clasping lips. She held it there, not breathing, looking up at him, her master — the one who had granted her this brief favour, this short moment of delectable pleasure.

She rocked forward very slowly, and then rocked back in the same way. He did not move and I saw the shaft of his cock glistening with her spit as it was withdrawn from her black-lipped mouth. He dropped his right hand behind her head and pulled her down onto it. Again it filled her throat. This time he held her there and she waited obediently until the time he would decide to release her. In the end, her salvation came. Casually, he removed his hand and drew back. His still-hard cock slipped out and I stared at its glistening venous surface as Sublime struggled for breath.

She stayed on her knees as spit ran down in long gluey strands from her gaping mouth.

He beckoned me forward.

'On your hands and knees.'

I went down on all fours and crawled towards him.

'Slowly. There is no rush to repentance. Think of what you are doing. Let each rising hand remind you of your sins, let each scraping knee bring back the flavour of your evil ways. Think, as you approach me, how you have transgressed, how you have sought your own pleasure, allowed yourself to be punished just so that the fever of joy would be released from within you. Do not rush to my feet, for there will be little pleasure for you once you arrive.'

I slowed down even more as I heard his ominous words. I measured the pace of my approach carefully and, each time I lifted my hand or moved my knees forward, I thought again of the ways I had been filled with pleasure at the hands of those who punished me. I reminded myself of the degradation and shame that I had been exposed to and how, no matter what depths of humiliation I had been drawn down to, I had still been rent by the heat in my cunt and the fire of my own burning orgasms. I felt a wave of shame and the need to repent.

I looked down at Athala's bare feet as I came nearer. I hoped he would allow me to lick them, to drip my spit on them, to feel them against my lips. Perhaps I might be able to bite at his toenails, or lick between his toes, or press my eyes against the prominent bones of his ankles. Or, more rightly, he might not let me do any of those things, and I would be forced only to imagine the pleasure of being held back, restrained from seeking out the joy of my uncontrolled desires. I shivered all over as I realised there was no way out of the trap in which I found myself — punishment gave me pleasure in the same way that having potential punishment withheld gave me pleasure. I was truly a sinner — ensnared in a paradox of ecstasy. Surely there was no salvation for someone like me.

'You have been suffering, my child, and taking your pleasures with your pain. I will try and exorcise you of your evil. I will try and bring out the devil of pleasure which hides behind every lash, every scream, and every degrading humiliation to which you are subject.'

I stopped at his feet. I wanted to bend my lips towards them. I would have been content with just that. I did not know if I could stand the ecstasy of actual contact with his skin. I waited expectantly.

'Follow!' he ordered.

He turned and strode off into the darkness. I crawled behind him, each movement of my hips squeezing the softness of my cunt, each reach of my arms exerting extra tension against the throbbing aching in my nipples.

His robe swirled around his feet as he walked up several steps onto a rostrum. He turned back, pulled his robe open and dropped down onto a heavy stone throne. He let his legs fall wide apart. His cock was still hard, the slow throbbing of his erection bulging out the heavy veins which ran up its massive shaft.

'You may not come nearer. Lie on your back and open your legs. I will look at your naked cunt for a while and decide exactly how you should be punished. I need to select something which will cause only pain, from which you cannot release your own pleasure and need. Lie on your back. I must ponder the problem.'

I did as he said — there was no alternative. I felt completely under his control. I looked up at the dark roof of the cavern — it flashed with the shimmering light of the torches which were placed around the walls. I opened my legs, aware that I was exposing my cunt fully to his gaze, and that it would be his seeing of it which dictated my punishment. I felt moisture on my flesh and knew that its soft surface was glistening in the light of the torches.

I watched the flickering reflections on the roof as what seemed an age passed in silence. I thought I heard him leave his throne for a while, and I thought I saw a shadow cast across my body, but I did not take my gaze from where I had fixed it on the roof. I felt committed to carry out only his instructions. Shadows told me that others moved nearby, but still I forced myself to look only upwards.

Suddenly, my hands were being held, my fingers were being prised open. Then something was forced across each of my palms, and I saw a fresh set of shadows flickering wildly on the dark roof. A torch had been placed in each of my hands. I felt the heat from the spluttering flames and hot, sparkling shards of fire spewed from them and fell around my arms.

Then I felt bodies crouched by my legs. I did not dare look down. My ankles were grabbed. My legs were spread wide. Thin cords were tied around them and these were secured by metal pins driven into the ground. I flinched every time the hammer banged against the metal spikes. My cunt was fully exposed — I imagined its wetness glittering in the flickering light. I gripped the torches tightly in my hand. Still I did not move.

I lay beneath the sparking flames of the torches — naked and exposed to the dark shadowy figures that surrounded me, my cunt open and bare, my nipples hard and throbbing as the hot glittering embers from the torches showered down upon them. I was terrified.

'Now, my child, we shall see if there is a way of punishing you without releasing your pleasure. We shall see if the flames of your own desire can indeed be quelled by the fires of suffering.'

I stared up at the roof — shadowy images danced across its uneven rock surface. I knew I must not look away — it was part of my test.

'Let the test begin!'

There was no pause, no time to prepare. I saw a fleeting shadow on the roof, and then I felt the cutting slap of a leather belt brought down squarely across the exposed flesh of my cunt. I did not know whether I felt pain or surprise, whether I was filled with fear or horror. I only knew I must keep the torches in my hands and my eyes firmly fixed on the shadowy ceiling of rock above me.

The next came down, and the next, and the next. Each time I saw a fleeting glimpse of shadows, a sense of movement in the torchlight, but nothing more. The pain was intense — it penetrated me so deeply, every part of me was burned by it, every nerve I had was scorched by it. Surely this was pure pain. It could serve no other purpose than to inflict hurt.

Sparks flew from the torches in a storm of flashing shards. I gripped them as hard as possible. I never moved — not for a second did I give in to the lacerating pain that the belt brought to my exposed cunt. But my inability to respond spelled my doom. I did not have to move. I did not have to squirm or rise up to the cutting belt. I did not have to lift my hips to meet it, or tighten my buttocks to feel the squeezing pressure on my flesh. It was enough that the pain was there, that I was enduring it, that there was no escape, no relief, no promise that it would end. It was enough that I was secured by my ankles, and that my hands were gripping the torches. It was enough that my ankles were held fast by the ropes and pins, and that my hands were held fast by my own obligation to do as I was instructed. And, as the belt came down time after time, and I stared at the flickering images on the ceiling, and the sparks spluttered from the fiery torches, I felt the heat of my own desire burning inside me. I don't know where it started — it was impossible to tell, I was too racked with pain to tell — but it spread throughout me and centred on the vicious pain that covered and penetrated the soft flesh of my cunt. I tried to hold my breath — to keep it back — but it was a pointless effort. I bit my lips, I let my mouth fill with spit, I pressed my tongue against the back of my teeth, but nothing held it back. Suddenly, I opened my mouth. It was like a demon escaping. Breath burst from me. It was released like an explosion and, as the belt came down again and again — thrashing the flesh of my cunt, opening it more, bruising it, setting it on fire — my own joy flooded through me and I drowned beneath its tormenting, unstoppable surge.

It was raining hard as I walked slowly down to the iron gate that led out onto the road. I dropped the latch behind me — it clanked like a cell door. I felt as if I had been released early from a prison, as if my sentence had been commuted, as if I was a hopeless case, rejected as impossible to rehabilitate. I had not looked back, but had left the tomb of Athala feeling only despondent and dejected. It seemed as though I was truly beyond redemption. It seemed as though no pain or suffering could hold back my pleasure. The beating had continued but it had only released more joy. My ecstasy had grown as it had continued and I had screamed out with delight as I lay unmoving beneath the torrent of cutting blows.

Rain dripped from the end of my nose and off my chin as I leant against the curving wall that bordered the cemetery.

I saw some figures approaching — it was the small group of runners I had seen earlier. The beautiful Oriental girl was still at the front. Their heavy swatches of hair bobbed from side to side as they approached. The group paused. The Oriental girl smiled and looked at her watch.

'You were not too long,' she said. 'I will check you out

at 3.30. Safe to carry on now. Goodbye. Come on, patrol.'

She waved to the group and together they started running again.

I watched them jogging along the pavement that ran alongside the long snaking wall of the cemetery. I realised that they were not just passing runners, they were a patrol, guarding the perimeter to the cemetery and what it enclosed. They had checked me in and checked me out. I could not be the only one seeking the treatment of Athala. I was filled with dread as a thought occurred to me. Could I be the only one for whom it did not work?

15. VERMONT
THE CALIMNITES

I felt I had to go north, I don't know why. Perhaps it was the increasing coldness, the greenness, and the remoteness that drew me on. Perhaps I felt every mile further north took me further away from something I did not understand — my need for humiliation, for pain, and for the suffering dealt out by a cruel master. And, as I travelled away from the midday sun, I felt as if things were drawing to an end — as if I was getting closer not further away, as if some resolution was at last in sight. And here I was in Vermont, and I did not know why.

Vermont — rolling hills covered with forests of maple, birch and spruce: in summer, a brilliant display of green; in fall, a blaze of flaming colour; in winter, a bare and endless expanse freezing beneath deep snow. Vermont — quaint cedar clapboard houses with sharply pitched roofs, no fences, no property separation, and no premium on land. Vermont, strewn with bookshops, organic vegetables, flowers, palmists, and hunters — gentility and cruelty, uncomfortable partners forced together and inbred. Vermont — truly a land lost in the new ages.

I sat in the Cooperative Café in Hardwick — a haven of organic food, quietness, civility and calm. A woman with long dark hair stared purposefully into the open hands of a girl who stood before her as if presenting herself for inspection. The girl's bright pink, silky shorts, white vest, white socks and pink trainers, contrasted with the earthy beiges and browns of her surroundings.

The dark haired woman flexed the girl's two outstretched and out-turned thumbs. She frowned and shook her head.

'What does it mean?' asked the girl, as she raised her right foot and used the closely tied laces of her trainers to scratch the back of her firm left thigh just above the top of her sock.

The dark haired woman frowned again as though she was straining to decipher a hidden code.

'Tell me! Tell me!' whinnied the girl as she jumped up and down and bent her knees with uncontrollable excitement. 'Tell me! I shall die if you don't!'

She pulled her hands free and clapped them together then, realising what she had done, she stretched them out and again presented them, palm up, to scrutiny.

I was captivated by the girl's energy, her enthusiasm for life, and her keenness to know her own future. How could she wish to know what was ahead of her, I thought? How could she be so naive? I could not look away from her bright and eager eyes — their sparkle fixated me.

'Captivating isn't she?'

A man's voice — deep and silky — caused me to jump and turn around in surprise.

He was a mature man, craggy faced, tanned, dark haired and dressed in jeans and a loose, faded red T shirt. He smiled. I raised my eyebrows and smiled back. I pushed my hands between my legs and flushed with embarrassment as my fingers glanced the insides of my thighs — my skirt was short and I had no panties on. And, as I looked down, I noticed that only two of the buttons of my shirt were done up.

'No need to feel embarrassed,' he said. I flushed even more. 'I saw you had no panties on the moment you sat down. And I saw that you shave your pubic hair as well. I saw that your cunt was smooth and naked. Did you want to show me, or was it just my good luck?'

'I didn't mean…' I started, but I sounded ridiculous.
'Just luck then, eh?'
'Yes, I suppose…'

I felt my face going red.

'So, do you find her captivating? She's not as young as she looks, you know. They keep them like that.'

I raised my eyebrows.

'Keep them like that?'

'Yes, the Calimnites. They like their women to look young. They like a lot of things that would surprise those outside the faith.'

I put my hands on my knees. I felt them trembling.

He looked at them and smiled knowingly.

'I could tell you things that would really make you tremble. What do you think? Would you like me to?'

I was nodding before I even thought about his question.

'Yes, please,' I said, for a moment feeling as naive and eager as the young girl.

'Well, first of all, this place is owned by them. Don't look now, but the woman who served you is one of their ministers. And the girl, well, she was a cheerleader when I first saw her. What a dream. I followed her the first time to a roadside café, just to watch her — delectable. After that I could not stop — I tracked her everywhere. When she was out with her friends, I followed her and watched her laughing, chatting, and sipping milk shakes through straws. When she went swimming, I stared at her in her tight, thin, salmon pink, one piece costume as she went slowly backwards down the pool steps and entered the water. That costume. The material was so sheer, so skimpy; I could see every part of her beautiful lithe body through it. Can you imagine that? I went to every game but saw only her — waving her purple pompoms, small beads of sweat on her forehead, prancing like a young pony, the flesh of her sweet cunt pulled tightly inside the material of her high-cut, mauve coloured panties. I found a place on some scaffolding where I could see into the changing rooms. I can hardly bear to describe it. I crouched there with my cock in my hand — throbbing, hard, and aching. I squeezed it so tightly as I saw her peel off her tight vest, drop her silky yellow-hemmed skirt to the ground, and stand, glowing with youthful beauty in her bra, panties, socks and trainers. Seeing her bend to undo her laces made me drool — literally. Spit actually ran over my bottom lip. I pulled on my cock as I watched her, aching for the ecstasy of a climax, yet dreading that it should come too soon. I stared between her tight buttocks as she bent, my eyes fixed on the gusset of her panties, indented in a shallow valley where it pressed against the centre of her cunt. I watched it squeezing against her flesh as she moved from side to side — massaging it, stroking it, testing its delectable pliability. I just wanted to reach forward and lick it — to lay the flat of my tongue against the fragrant material. And when she undid her bra — unclipped it at the back, between her well-defined shoulder blades — and her firm youthful breasts were exposed, I could only close my eyes. I could not stand looking at their magnificent taut shape, their roundness, their firm succulence, and the way they moved in tune with the rest of her body. And her beautiful nipples — hard, pink, extended, urgent with desire. I saw my lips around them, my tongue against their ends — sucking them, taking their prominent hardness into my mouth, tasting them, feeding from her delectable sweetness. And, as my head spun with it all, I knew what was next. The billowing steam from the showers was already curling around her now naked ankles as it dropped to the ground. It was as if it crawled on the floor in submission, as if it sought out the cooler air next to its surface which did not dare rise above her feet. Or perhaps, I thought, it swirled low and feigned its submissive position in the hope of finding a better view up between her thighs to her still- covered cunt. I felt the pulsating veins in my cock straining against my clutching hand as, finally, she pulled her panties down — first one leg slightly bent, then the other simply lifted. And she bent to touch something on her toes — perhaps a snagged nail, or a strand of cotton from her socks. Just think of it. And the delectable oval of her pink cunt appeared between her upturned buttocks — soft and pliable, closely defined, slightly dark at its centre, peachy, smooth, and glistening. I gripped my cock and spit drooled all down my chin. The sensations were impossible to contain. Everything about her was completely overwhelming. As my semen splattered into my hand, as I continued to grip the shaft of my pulsating cock and, as I watched her running with her naked friends into the billowing steam of the showers, I knew I would never be released from her spell — I was a pitiful subject of her beauty.

The man shuffled up closer. I felt the heat of his body against my thighs. His sallow swarthiness and tall muscular bearing made him magnetically attractive.

'You don't mind, do you? Me sitting closer?'

'No, not at all,' I said, my voice trembling breathlessly from the excitement of his story.

He patted his hand on my knee. I felt another shiver of excitement. It only added to the excitement already caused by his captivating tale. I had to lick my lips, and I felt myself slurping. I felt my cheeks reddening.

'The next thing I knew,' he continued, 'was that she was moving — her family had decided to seek a quieter life in Vermont. I used to sit in a tree in their yard watching her write in her diary — she was often naked, or just wore her white cotton, high-cut panties. I was sure she did not want to leave.'

'What did you do?' I asked, sniffing in a ridiculous way to disguise licking my lips again.

'There was only one thing I could do — I followed. Almost straight away they got involved with the Calimnites, going to their meetings, dressing Shona — that's her name, by the way, I quite forgot to say — dressing Shona in the way they liked: young looking, no make-up, usually no panties, no pubic hair of course, short cropped hair. She was not allowed to do any cheerleading, naturally, though secretly she still kept up with her exercises. I used to crouch beneath her bedroom windowsill and watch as she bent and stretched naked beside her bed. After she had mopped herself with a towel, she would kneel and pray — leaning her elbows against the edge of the quilt-covered bed, her hands clasped together, her eyes closed, and her lips barely moving — as she repeated the lines she had been taught.

'It was no trouble to watch what went on at the Calimnites' meetings. Although someone always guarded the entrance to their meeting hall, it was easy to slip in through a back door. I was never seen, it was always only half lit anyway. Here, they lined up their daughters, always in a row, one behind the other facing their simple altar. Each one was taken for communion in turn. Shona was last in the line to start with but, as time went on, as she herself brought more girls into the congregation — for she was a keen worker — she moved up until she was only several places from the front. I could tell by the bright glint in her eye that her object was to become the girl who headed the row.'

'What did they do?'

'What do they do? They still do it. Come with me. I'll show you.'

We left the café. I thought the woman behind the till scowled at me as I paid. The man led me through a door into a barely lit room. The sound of our footsteps echoed around us as we walked in.

'It's okay,' he said. 'No one will disturb us in here.'

He pulled up two chairs and we both sat facing each other. He leant forward and rested his hands on my knees — his palms on their tops, his thumbs on the insides. I felt a slight pressure pushing my knees apart. I allowed it, and felt a delightful coolness of air against the soft, warm flesh of my cunt.

'Each one in the queue — you remember, the queue of girls — each one was led behind the altar and made to kneel. The minister was a tall man — black haired and lean. He would place his hands on the girl's head. "Let me save you my child," he would say. "Let me save you from your sins."'

I felt the pressure of his thumbs increasing as he spoke. It was as though uttering these particular words excited him — inflamed him.

'What happened next?' I asked.

'Shh,' he said. 'I will tell you. Better, I can show you. Here, kneel down.' He stood up. 'Here, right here. I'll show you.'

I looked from side to side hurriedly, as if there was someone there who could tell me what to do. I felt a wave of nerves in my stomach. I knew I shouldn't do it.

I knelt on the floor in front of him. I squeezed my buttocks together. The soft flesh of my cunt throbbed with excitement.

'Now, put your hands together,' he said. 'Yes, just like that.'

He placed his hands on my head. I could feel the heat from his palms. My nipples tingled as they hardened and pressed against the material of my shirt. I squeezed my buttocks together again and felt a sudden shiver of excitement run from my cunt right up into my pounding chest.

'Let me save you, my child,' he boomed. 'Let me save you from your sins.'

I gulped. The image of Father Dawson flashed into my mind. I saw myself again in the desert, tied to the post, waiting for my thrashing, waiting to be excused my sins. The image blurred. I felt myself panting. I was filled with a fluttering nervous anticipation of what might happen next.

'I'll show you,' he said. 'I'll show you how they treated my darling Shona. How they made her suffer. Here, come forward. No! Do not walk! Stay on your knees! Come to this table on all fours. You can rest your elbows on it. It will help.'

I moved forward on my knees. They scuffed on the rough timber planks. I got to the edge of the table — I hadn't even seen it. There was a white cloth draped over it. I rested my elbows on it as he had instructed.

'Good. Now, just think of yourself as one of those girls — one of those girls who shaves her pubic hair, who keeps her cunt naked just for the pleasure of leering men. Think of yourself as one of them, dressing in a short skirt, never wearing panties, hoping all the time that you will be able to show your naked crack to any man who is sitting opposite from you.'

My mind was filled with the picture he painted. It was as if he had hypnotised me. I felt exactly like one of the girls — wanton, wilful and wayward. And I knew that now I would have to pay for this terrible sin I had committed — the sin of disporting myself, enjoying the prying eyes of a man on my cunt, encouraging his stare by widening my knees.

'I can see you know it,' he said. 'I can see you realise your sinfulness. Now, you must receive the sacrament which I can only hope will allow you to be forgiven.'

He lifted a silver bowl from the table.

'Here, hold this in your hands.'

I took the bowl and held it in my cupped palms. He looked down at me, and I dropped my head in submission.

Someone walked out of the darkness — a man clothed in a white robe.

'Hold the bowl before him.'

I turned and did as I was instructed.

The man opened his robe and exposed his hard cock.

'Now fill the bowl with his fluid.'

I reached forward and took the tip of the hard cock in my mouth. I licked my tongue around it then drove my head forward onto it. I felt it touch the back of my throat, and I felt it swell as it detected the extra tightness. I felt its throbbing increase, and I tasted the first droplets of semen as they began flowing up its burgeoning shaft. I just tasted before I took my mouth away and let it splash into the bowl. I reached out and squeezed it to make sure I did not miss a drop.

Another man came forward and then another. I treated each the same, although I kept some of them in my mouth too long and had to empty some of their semen from my mouth into the bowl.

I don't know how many came forward — how many I took in my mouth, how many added their gluey semen to the contents of my bowl — but I knew it was enough when the man who had taken me to the room told me to place the bowl back on the table.

I did as I was told, and waited. There was semen on my hands and some of it dripped from my lips. I did not know whether he would allow me to lick it back into my mouth so I did nothing, I just left it there and waited.

He stepped forward, undid my shirt, drew it from my shoulders and tossed it aside. He unbuttoned my skirt at the side and released the waistband. He draped a white silk tassel-edged shawl over my bare shoulders.

'Now you may take the sacrament. Lift the bowl to your lips and drink the wine of the Calimnites.'

I lifted the bowl and held it in front of my mouth — it was brimful of semen. My mouth dropped open — I needed it so much. I placed the edge of the silver bowl against my lips and tipped it until I could feel the surface of delectable fluid. It was like a magical sea — spreading out before me to the horizon. I shivered with excitement as I opened my lips and sucked it in.

It was thick and glutinous as I sucked it up. I tipped the bowl further until my mouth was filled. I held it there for a moment — on my tongue and inside my cheeks. Then I swallowed it down slowly. I did not gulp it, I restrained my greediness and managed to hold back my desire to guzzle it down with uncontrolled thirst. It went down my throat in a long silky stream. I felt it go all the way and I felt it rest in my stomach. But straight away, I needed more of the salty tang, the silky consistency, and the filling sensation it gave me. I tipped the bowl further and slurped at it noisily. I swallowed each mouthful eagerly until I was full and the bowl was empty. I licked around the edges and poked my tongue around the inside until it was completely clean.

I held the bowl up to him to show him that I had taken the sacrament, that I had drained every drop and was now filled with it — satiated, heavy with its burden.

He looked inside the bowl, checking that it was empty.

'And do you want more, my child?'

I nodded slowly. I opened my mouth but could not speak — I was too excited, too fragile. Semen trickled down my chin. I held my tongue out. He took it between his thumb and forefinger and pinched it. I closed my mouth and sucked at his fingers. He pinched harder and I sucked harder. Spit and semen bubbled from my mouth, frothing down his fingers and running down my chin and onto the front of my throat.

He raised me up by my tongue. I stood and my skirt fell around my ankles. He drew my head forward and leant me down across the communion table. With his other hand he lifted the white robe and exposed my naked bottom. Still pinching my tongue and holding me in place using the grip he had on it, he brought the flat of his other hand down squarely on my bottom.

It smacked loudly and I tensed against it, but the tension did not remain in my buttocks; it transmitted itself directly to my cunt and a wave of excitement ran through me. I slurped on his thumb and finger, and sucked at them, and on the frothing semen and spit that still ran around them. Another smack and I tasted more, another and I felt my cunt heating up, another and I felt the heat from it spreading throughout my body, another and I began to feel the shiver of excitement that I knew would lead me unerringly to the full joy of my own ultimate and irrepressible ecstasy.

He pinched harder each time he smacked, and my mind was filled with my own slurping, the taste of semen, the pain in my tongue and the burning smacks across my upturned bottom. There was nothing else in my world — I was consumed by it all. Suddenly, I felt a jerk come on me then another and, as the rhythm of pain increased in tempo, the jerks merged into one and I was overtaken by the thundering roar of my coursing blood and the pounding of my frantically beating heart,

Suddenly, the lights went on. The room was full of people! Shona was standing by the dark haired woman who had been reading her palm in the café. A great cheer went up and they all started clapping, then they burst into a hymn — clasping each other's arms and rocking from side to side in time with their chanting dirge. The hymn subsided and the clapping broke out again and, this time, built to a deafening crescendo. For a moment I thought their adulation was for me, but I felt my face flush red as I realised how stupid I was to think such a thing. I was simply a vehicle for someone else's glory.

Shona was pushed forward and, as other girls walked out and formed a line, Shona was directed proudly to its head. She had been rewarded for baiting the latest victim — me!

They did not try to hold me back — I was free to go — but, as I walked out of the packed room, their jeers, derision and contemptuous glances filled my head. I walked between them as they taunted me with comments, poked at me and spat on me. Semen dribbled from my lips and I hung my head, but the walk to the door seemed to take an age. I gripped the handle and turned back before opening it. I saw all the faces shouting, and I heard their mocking comments and, as I twisted the handle in my hand, I felt again a wave of joy as a fresh and powerful orgasm seized me with a sudden jerking wrench.

16. NIAGARA
FALL FROM GRACE

It was a slow drive on the I190 past Buffalo and into Canada. The queue at the immigration post was long and tedious and the beak-nosed uniformed immigration officer was facetious and tiresome. Suddenly life seemed duller, gas was more expensive, and everyone appeared to be either coming out of a long winter or preparing to enter the next one.

I arrived at Niagara Falls, parked the pick-up and walked to the Canadian Horseshoe to see if I could find the spot where Superman rescued Lois Lane from the horror of drowning in the roaring falls below.

Niagara Falls — tall, tower block hotels, crowds of tourists, the endless thunder of the falls, everything tacky and gaudy. I sat outside a café staring across to the American Falls — gigantic, forceful, smashing down in uncontrolled torrents on the jagged rocks below. I watched anxious newlyweds clinging to each other like octopuses — unable to move away from each other's grasp, unable to release the other for fear of falling down in a dizzy turn of separation. Somehow, I knew this was the end of my journey. Somehow, I knew I would travel no further north.

A young woman, barely in her mid teens, sat with a muscular young man a few years older than her, on a high-backed bench looking out towards the falls. Occasionally the mist rose up in a huge cloud, was caught by a sudden gust of wind, and blew across them in a drenching shower. The girl's skin, smooth and moistened, radiated youth and naivety. But her eager smiles, and the way she clutched the muscular arm of what looked a new and more mature husband, testified to the sexual heat which had been ignited in her slender, taut body. She wore a very short skirt. The flimsy material clung to her buttocks — tightly drawn together, compact, firm yet pliable. I imagined her cunt — malleable, soft, and wet — and I heard myself breathing heavily.

Her husband got up and went to a nearby counter for food. The girl looked across and smiled at me. I smiled back. She tossed her head back and opened her mouth. I saw her pink tongue, glinting and wet with moisture, as her full broad lips opened wide. It was as if she allowed me to look inside for a few moments, then, when she thought I had seen enough, she closed her lips together again and offered me another broad smile.

She glanced at her husband. He was searching for money in the rear pocket of his tight jeans. The straining tension of his hand in the pocket pulled the worn, blue material tightly against his prominent cock and outlined the general shape of his weighty testicles.

She jumped up and quickly came over to me.

'My name's Angela. Tonight, 8pm, Maid of the Mist. Meet me there.'

She squeezed my hand and went back to her table. She did not look at me again after her husband returned, preoccupied as she was — petting him and kissing his tanned cheeks and neck, laying her hand on his lap, and fingering his cock within the tight creases of his jeans.

When she got up to leave, she opened her knees to slide herself across the seat — I thrilled at the briefest glimpse of her naked cunt. I felt the pounding beats of my heart in my neck.

I sat around thinking of what Angela had said, and how she had said it — the air of mystery and the hint of knowing, both mixed together and spoken with a voice of naivety and innocence. The words of the old Indian woman who had stopped me when I had escaped from Father Dawson came back into my mind. She had said that the place I would find grace would be 'where a young woman will lead you into the mist'. A sudden wave of fear ran through me. It was as though I was meeting my fate — acting out a part in a drama beyond my control, a destiny that had been mapped out for me by others who I did not even know. The thought unsettled me and I felt nervous and uncomfortable.

I walked around the town impatiently and, eventually, at 8pm, I found myself on the promenade above the dock for the Maid of the Mist. I stared down at the heavily built boats which transport tourists in blue plastic raincoats to only yards beneath the crashing and relentless torrent of the Niagara horseshoe. The ticket offices were closed. There was no one to be seen.

Someone grabbed my arm from behind. I swung around. It was Angela.

'Come down here,' she said, dragging me urgently by the hand.

I didn't have time to think as we went quickly down a long tunnel carved into the rock. We passed a young girl pressed against the wall by a thrusting boy. She wrapped her legs around his buttocks and pulled his hard cock into her needy cunt with forceful desperate jerks. She reminded me of someone, but I did not know who. I slowed to watch.

'Ignore them,' said Angela. 'Come on!'

She squeezed my hand tightly and rushed on into the tunnel. We passed a naked woman on her hands and knees. She did not move as we ran by.

'She's waiting for her master's orders,' said Angela. 'Come on! Come on!'

We rounded a corner. A woman was chained by the wrists, face forward against the rough rock wall. She was stripped naked. Her clothing lay in an untidy pile by her feet. Her back and buttocks were covered in raw red stripes. Her head hung limply onto her shoulder — her mouth gaping, spit running from its corners. A man wearing only leather jeans flogged her with a short broad leather whip. She looked unconscious and no longer aware of the pain that had driven her to this state of senselessness.

'Hurry! Hurry!'

Angela pulled me along. We passed a small tunnel leading off to the right — I heard the sound of a flogging strap and the high pitched screams of pain it wrung from its victim. Somewhere, I could not tell exactly the direction or location, I heard the endless scream of another suffering soul whose punishment I could only imagine. I shivered as pictures of her horrendous torture and humiliation sprang into my mind. I imagined her being crucified and could not shake the thought from my head.

'We're here! Here, put this on.'

Angela held out a long, blue, plastic raincoat. It was made of very thin plastic, translucent, with a hood and wide cape-like arms. On the back was written "Maid of the Mist".

'Put this on. You'll need it!'

I took it from her and began to pull it over my head.

'Take your clothes off first!' I looked at her and she nodded vigorously. 'Yes! Yes! Take them all off. And be quick!'

I pulled my T shirt over my head, undid my jeans and

pulled them, together with my light green panties, down to my feet. I stepped out of them and kicked them into a pile against the rock wall. I struggled for a moment to work out how to get the plastic raincoat over my head. When, finally, I pulled it down, its thin filmy surface stuck to my skin. I could see my breasts through it, and my hard nipples stood out prominently against it. It clung between my thighs and the shape of my naked cunt was outlined and completely visible. I pulled the hem down as well as I could, as Angela grabbed my hand again and dragged me on.

We ran out into the open and down a metal gangway with worn wooden handrails. The sound of the falls was all around us. I could see the mist billowing from the massive horseshoe on the Canadian side, and a low, arched rainbow buried itself in the crashing torrent opposite on the American side.

She led me up onto the Maid of the Mist.

'Here! Stand here!' She pulled me to the iron rails which bounded the bow of the boat. 'Yes, here. I will help you. Quickly!'

A heavy stanchion, a sort of mast, rose up from the grey teak deck. Wet ropes hung from either sides of a crossbar welded to the heavy upright at shoulder height. She stood me in front of it and pressed me back against the rusty iron mast. It was rough and cold, and I shivered as she drew out my arms and began tying my wrists to the ropes which hung from the cross bar.

She drew the ropes up tightly — I winced as she leant back and yanked on them with her full weight. When she had finished, she dropped to her knees, placed my ankles either side of the upright stanchion and tied them securely with more rope. My ankles bones were pulled against the rough and rusty iron and I shouted out in pain. She took no notice, but put even more pressure on the rope as if she was punishing me for my weakness.

I hung on the cross bar, slightly twisted at the waist as I allowed some of my weight to hang on my wrists. I flexed my hands and felt how securely I was tied. Then, as if I had not noticed what had happened to me, I had a sudden surge of fear as I realised my situation, and I saw how I had so quickly allowed myself to be put in it. The image I had of the crucified screaming woman flashed into my mind and I dropped against the ropes at my wrists as if accepting my fate.

Angela pressed herself against the rails at the point of the bow and stared ahead. Suddenly, I remembered what the old Indian woman had said — the place where a girl would 'lead me into the mist'. Yes, this must be where the old woman had predicted my sins would be washed away. For a moment, I wondered if I dared submit to my salvation, but I realised that I already had, I was bound to the crucifying crossbeam and already we were heading into the roaring waters of the massive waterfall ahead. Yes, this was where, at last, I would be redeemed.

The mist covered my face. At first it was a soft and caressing moisture, but soon it became a violent storm. The plastic raincoat stuck to my body. I looked down at my breasts and nipples, and my navel and, beyond that, the outline of my cunt — I could see its pink nakedness through the filmy blue plastic. I felt the pressure of the tugging wet surface on my skin. I moved myself against it, and felt a wave of joy spread to every rain-soaked pore of my body.

The hood dropped down and partly covered my face. Water battered me in a heavy and massive deluge. I could hardly breathe as it pounded against my face and chest. It ran in a stream down the gully formed by the thin plastic pulled tightly between my thighs. Everything around me was in turmoil. The ship pitched and rocked in the white churning waters that surrounded it. The hood dropped further down until it stuck to my nose. I could see nothing clearly.

I saw Angela moving ahead in the mist. I think she stood up and turned and, suddenly, out of nowhere, I thought I saw the old Indian woman beckoning me, reaching out to me, calling me to her. I strained against the ropes at my wrists and tried to shout to her, but it was useless, any sound I made was drowned by the roaring thunder of the falls.

There was only whiteness around me — I was entombed in the thundering mist of the falls. I could not see where I was, which way was up and which way down. I felt as if I was drowning.

I thought I saw Father Dawson's two penitents running, like ghouls, through the swirling spray. Again I shouted, but this time I could not even hear myself as my mouth filled with water the instant I opened it.

My mind was full of images. I thought I was delirious. I saw a flying eagle, and then Bracken flying through the rain. I thought I felt Sir Orfeo's touch, or his bite, around my nipples — I even winced in pain. I blinked my eyes and held them wide in fear. I felt a rush of humiliation as I thought I saw Leanne and Crystal. It was as though all the people I had met on my travels were appearing before me, as if they were on a stage, and nothing I could do would stop them. If I closed my eyes they were there, and if I opened them they seemed only the more real. May from Johnson's Farm stood before me beckoning, smiling, peeling off her clothes, and Petra and Robin reached forward and placed their hands across my eyes, giggling, wanting to play a game with me. I thought I saw Dr Fitz bending and clasping my nipples between his teeth, and I even saw the flash of Sublime's green hair crest, just before I felt the stinging lash of Athala's cane on my bottom. I felt giddy and confused. The burning taste of vomit welled up in my throat. The hood of the raincoat was stuck to my face, everything I saw was tinted blue and drenched with saturating spray. I struggled against my bonds and felt weakened by the effort. I slumped against the ropes at my wrists and hung on the crossbar terrified, confused and unsure what, if anything, was real. Then I saw the delectable Shona walking towards me arm in arm with Father Dawson! I gasped and my mouth filled with water.

He stood in the storm of spray and stared at me. He grinned and came closer. He pressed his face against my ear. He was real!

'Syra. My dearest Syra.'

He spoke! I couldn't believe it! I stared at him blankly.

'Have you been so long away from your master that you no longer recognise him? Poor Syra. Surely you didn't think you had actually escaped from me? Oh, Syra! Surely not! You did! Syra! You did! You actually thought you had found freedom. Oh, my dear Syra, I am embarrassed for you. You are such a fool! Syra, I have watched you all the way. Throughout your journey, you have been playing my game. What other game is there for you to play? Oh, my poor Syra. You have never been out of my sight. I have watched everything — everything!'

The plastic hood fell over my face. My heavy tears

mixed with the thunderous spray. His words shocked me with a pain as deep as any I had ever felt from the whip or belt or smacking hand. He was truly my nemesis — he was inescapable.

He backed away and Shona and Angela untied me from the mast. I felt I was being let down from the cross. I fell forward onto my hands and knees. I knew he was going to punish me, and I knew it would be worse than ever. I had committed the sin of thinking I could escape him and that could only be forgiven by more suffering at his hand. And I feared it but, at the same time, I wanted it. In the storm of spray and the thunderous roar of the waterfall, amid the dizzying confusion and the realisation of my own stupidity, I wanted salvation more than ever and that meant I wanted punishment.

I raised my bottom. The plastic clung to it. I felt him thrust his fingers against it and into my cunt. I felt as if the surface of my whole body was inside my cunt. The plastic pulled tight against my skin and his fingers dragged it close against my flesh. I raised my bottom more — it was the beginning of my punishment and I wanted it so much. The hood stuck across my mouth and I gasped as he thrust my cunt roughly. I moaned and cried out and whinnied and spit ran from my mouth and mixed with the vortex of water that churned around me. Suddenly, he took his fingers out. My jaw dropped. I felt empty — hollow without him inside me. But I waited. I knew he must thrash me. I knew I must kneel for the pain, take it all, and wait until he decided I had suffered enough — enough for repentance, enough to deliver me from the foolishness of believing there was such a thing as freedom outside his control — and only then would it be over.

The first lash made me cry out — it was so hard, so vicious. Spit foamed from my mouth and disappeared into the roaring vortex that surrounded me. I felt as though I was in a watery hell, drowning as I sacrificed myself to punishment. Another cutting blow. I was knocked forward but immediately put myself back in place, on my knees my bottom held as high as possible. That act of submission was enough to start it. I felt a jerk, a sudden jerk of pleasure, and knew it had begun. The next blow brought another, this time more intense, more directed, and I gritted my teeth and held myself ready for the next which was already following. I knew it would get worse, that the pain would only increase but, as the storm of spray whirled around me, and I realised that again I was on my knees before my master, I raised my bottom as I high as I could and hoped that, as he thrashed me, the edges of his belt would cut into the soft flesh of my cunt and deliver me to the ecstasy of repentance that my sins required.

I hung against the window of the fourteenth floor room of the Sheraton Fallsview Hotel. I stared out at the horseshoe of the falls as billowing mist curled from it in a massive incessant cloud. I looked down at the hectic, never-ending effort of valet parking around the entrance below. The gleaming bonnet of a shiny black Ford sedan flashed in my eyes. A man stepped out as the valet jumped into the driver's seat. The rear of the car dipped as, with a sudden squeal of tyres, it was driven away speedily. The man looked up. I could see it was him, even from this distance, I could see it was Father Dawson. He had left me in the hotel for the night to recover — he knew I would not run away, he knew I no longer believed in escape, even though I had been alone, he knew I had still been his prisoner. I had not even slept in the bed. I had curled up on the floor in anticipation of being put back again into my kennel at Dawson's Rise.

For a moment, I thought of waving to him, as though he was a friend who had come to collect me, but straight away I felt the stupidity of it. He had come to collect me, but not as a friend — he had come to collect his possession. He had let me run. He had let me imagine I was free and escaping my captivity, but it had only happened at his behest. He had arranged this mock freedom only to show me how much his prisoner I was, only to make me feel even more humbled by the let-down of realising that I had always been — that I always would be — in his clutches. In truth, I had never been out of his sight, and there was no point in pretending that he had found me, for I had never been lost.

The army of the Greeks is encamped outside the walls of Troy and the legendary war rages all around. So when Sappho and Chrysies, two beautiful Trojan girls are captured by their deadly enemies trying to flee the city, their situation is not a good one.

The question of who will possess and dominate the two slaves becomes the source of friction within the Greek camp and the two hapless captives can only pray that some miracle will help them escape from the cruel and warlike men into whose hands they have fallen.

As the great Trojan war moves towards its catastrophic end, the beautiful Trojan captives Sappho and Chryseis struggle to survive in the hostile camp of the Greeks. They are the helpless playthings of powerful men who fight each other for the spoils of war.

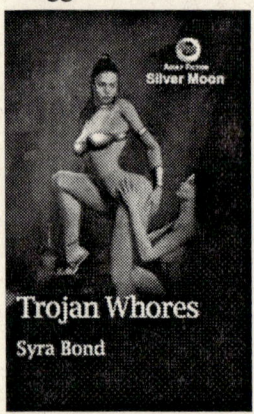

Praxis and Ajax, Achilles and Polydorus, slave traders and warriors alike want their share of the plunder from the ruins of Troy. The two girls are simply desirable flotsam to be exploited and used by whoever possesses them.

Suspected of the murder of her master, Syra was forced to go the run in the USA.

What followed was a sexual odyssey of extraordinary power and honesty. From adventure to adventure, Syra moves aimlessly across the States, always seeking fulfilment.

She meets a succession of dominant men and submissive women all of whom help her towards an understanding of her own nature.

Seductive hitch-hikers, a biker gang and a football team are among the people she meets, and they all help her explore her need for submission and suffering.

'True Confessions' is a stark and powerful work of erotica. Not to be missed!

There are over 100 stunningly erotic novels of domination and submission in the Silver Moon catalogue. You can see the full range, including Club and Illustrated editions by writing to:

Silver Moon Reader Services
Shadowline Publishing Ltd,
No 2 Granary House
Ropery Road,
Gainsborough,
Lincs. DN21 2NS

You will receive a copy of the latest issue of the Readers' Club magazine, with articles, features, reviews, adverts and news plus a full list of our publications and an order form.